The Prince

The Prince

Samhita Arni

juggernaut

JUGGERNAUT BOOKS
KS House, 118 Shahpur Jat, New Delhi 110049, India

First published by Juggernaut Books 2019

Map drawn by Saumya Sethia

10 9 8 7 6 5 4 3 2

This is a work of fiction. Any resemblance to persons, living or dead, or to actual incidents is purely coincidental.

ISBN 978-93-5345-022-9

Typeset in Adobe Caslon Pro by R. Ajith Kumar, Noida

Printed and bound at Thomson Press India Ltd

For my father

Cast of Characters

The Royals

From the dynasties and families of the three crowned kings of Tamilaham, the Cholas, Cheras and Pandyas

Nedum Cheralatan – king of the Cheras, rules in Vanchi, the city adjacent to the ancient port of Musiri

Karikala Chola – king of the Cholas, rules in Puhar, also known as Kaveripattinam

Nalchonai – queen of the Cheras, a Chola princess by birth, Karikala's sister and Uthiyan's mother

Shenguttuvan – crown prince of the Cheras, eldest son of Nedum Cheralatan with a Velir chieftain's daughter

Uthiyan – prince of the Cheras, second son of Nedum Cheralatan with Nalchonai

Neduncheliyan – king of the Pandyas, rules in Madurai

In addition to the kingdoms of the three crowned kings, there are a host of small rulers, who belong to the same dynasty – the Velirs – including the rulers of Aykudi, Tagadur, Parambu and Ilinji

Vel Pekan – chief of the Aviyar, ruler of Aykudi

Kannaki – Vel Pekan's wife and queen

Ilango Venmal – a Velir princess

Neduman Athiyaman Anji – ruler of Tagadur and patron of the famous poetess Avvaiyar

The Poets

Avvaiyar – poetess, patronized by Neduman Athiyaman Anji of Tagadur

Kapilar – poet, patronized by Vel Pekan and Vel Pari of Parambu

Paranar – poet, patronized by the Cheras and Vel Pekan

Others

Antuvan – a Chera soldier

Kannaki – a young woman from the Eyinar Maravar tribe

Kovalan – Kannaki's husband, son of a merchant in Puhar

Kavunthy – a female ascetic

Madhavi – a famous courtesan from Puhar

Sattan – the son of a merchant in Vanchi, a courtier at the Chera court and Uthiyan's best friend

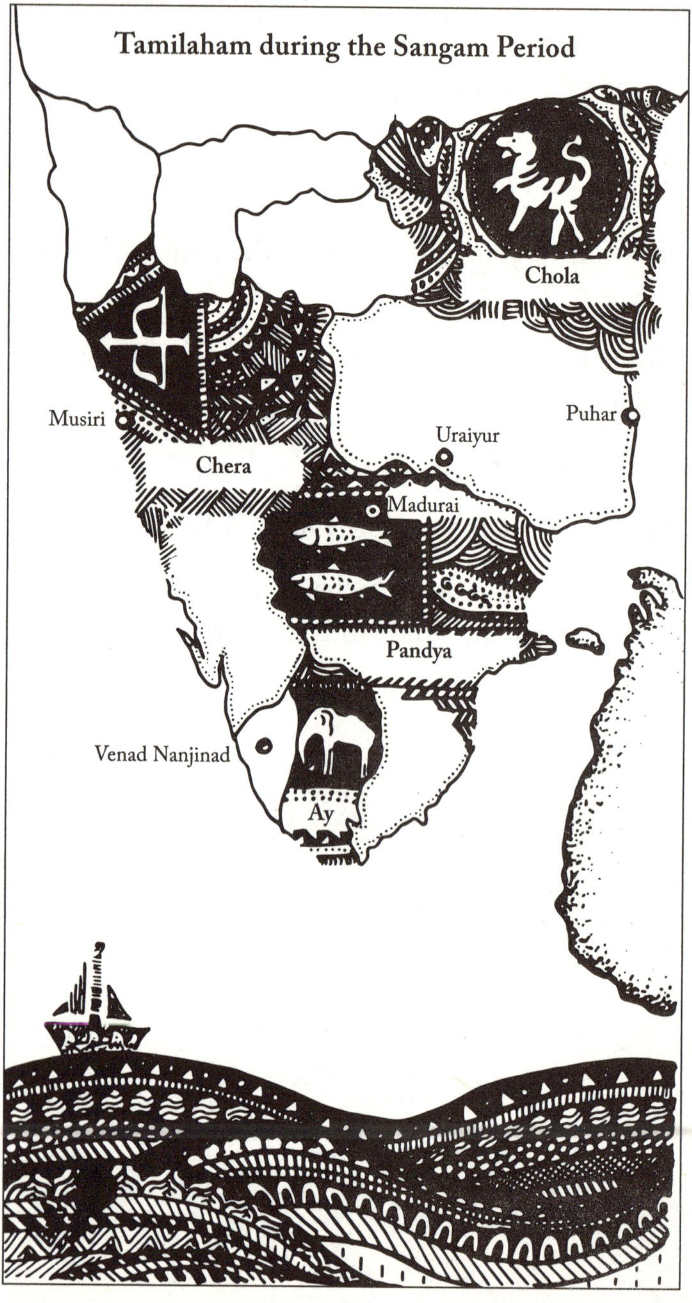
Tamilaham during the Sangam Period
Chola
Musiri
Puhar
Uraiyur
Chera
Madurai
Pandya
Venad Nanjinad
Ay

Book 1

Musiri

1

The most beautiful woman in the world was here in Vanchi, just a short distance – perhaps just a few scant metres – away from Uthiyan, but *when* would he get to see her? Stuck at his post in the chamber given over to the use of the royal scribes, Uthiyan bided his time.

To be the son of the king would have been the dream of most in the Chera kingdom, but to him the actual business of being the second son, Ilango, was to excel in being superfluous. Uthiyan loved composing poems and songs, and had no ability in the arts of the battlefield. For that reason the chief minister had advised the king that the best place for the spare prince was to be found in the department of the royal scribes, where his taste for the literary arts could be best employed in composing flowery, long-winded epistles to other kings and recording the duties paid on the cargoes of ships that came to the port of Musiri.

It was mind-numblingly boring. Each day, Uthiyan encountered the same murmured flatteries from the dutas – the emissaries, diplomats and messengers – sent from the other courts of Tamilaham. The same rustle of scrolls passed from one hand to the next, marked with the insignia of the twin fish, the eyes of the goddess of the kings to the north, the Pandyas. And then there were the letters from the queen's kin further away, those who fought under the sign of the leaping tiger, the Cholas; the crest that the queen's brother Karikala Chola was said to have engraved on the face of the Himalayas but – as the clerks who occupied the posts to either side of Uthiyan often snickered – no one had yet climbed the mountains to see it.

The only reprieve Uthiyan found was in the tales told by the interpreters who accompanied the Yavanas – the light-skinned men from across the seas, still smelling of the salty winds – of sea monsters and encounters with beautiful, cruel sorceresses who lived beneath the waves.

Uthiyan sprang from his seat when the hour came to a close, seeking to escape a persistent Yavana merchant with a cargo of red corals and wine, hoping to get his duties reduced by offering the prince a gift. He was cradling in his hands an object of the most exquisite workmanship, a lamp in the shape of a swan, that he told Uthiyan would be worth a small fortune even in his city, Rome. Uthiyan refused to entertain the merchant's request, as he knew his father would want him to, but couldn't help admiring the lamp. Such a thing, Uthiyan knew, would please his mother, who loved things of beauty.

Uthiyan thought of his mother then, ensconced in the Silver Palace in the pleasure gardens. And his mind went there, to the waterfalls that flashed like spun gold in the summer sun, to the thought of the groves filled with the sound of his mother's handmaidens, shrieking as they chased the green parrots that were forever escaping the finely wrought, impractical silver cages his mother kept them in.

And to the thought of her. Madhavi.

He had caught a distant glimpse of her yesterday, as she arrived from Puhar escorted by the Yavana bodyguard that the Chola king had assigned to protect this most beautiful jewel of his kingdom sent to entertain his sister in Vanchi.

Madhavi. It was as if the air spoke her name.

Madha-vvvvvi, the walls of the palace seemed to whisper.

This time, he could hear it.

He turned around swiftly and caught a faint quiver of movement behind a drapery. Uthiyan pulled it back to find Sattan, his best friend, grinning so hard that his face seemed in danger of splitting.

'Got you, didn't I?' Sattan chuckled. 'I hear she's practising. Come on, let's go!'

It didn't take much to persuade Uthiyan. They raced through the corridors of the palace, past startled courtiers and secretaries. As they rounded a corner and dashed past a group of soldiers, one reached out and yanked Uthiyan back by the edge of his waistcloth.

'Just where do you think you're both off to?'

Uthiyan looked up into the face of the Komahan, his elder brother Shenguttuvan. In shape and demeanour there couldn't be two brothers more unlike. Uthiyan was slim, delicate of feature, taking after his mother, Queen Nalchonai, a Chola princess before marriage. Shenguttuvan was muscular, brawny, like their father the king, Nedum Cheralatan. Uthiyan was dreamy and artistic, while Shenguttuvan had a reputation for being practical and shrewd. Perhaps the difference lay in the fact, as the courtiers often murmured, that Uthiyan came from more rarefied, genteel stock, while Shenguttuvan was of a coarser lineage; his mother, the king's first wife, had been a mere Velir chieftain's daughter. But the brothers were close despite their differences and dissimilar temperaments.

'The Perumdevi sent for us to welcome the courtesan Madhavi,' Sattan concocted a reason on the spot, knowing that Shenguttuvan, the conscientious crown prince, was likely to send them back to their duties.

'The great beauty? She's arrived?'

'Just last night,' Uthiyan replied breathlessly. 'Come with us.'

Shenguttuvan glanced back at his cohort, clearly torn.

'They say she is the most beautiful woman in the three kingdoms, brother,' Uthiyan craftily added.

'Oh, all right.' Shenguttuvan rolled his eyes. 'Just this once.'

2

The sound of the queen's musicians strumming the yal, the stringed lute, and striking the padalai, the one-sided drum, drew the trio to the inner courtyard in the centre of the Silver Palace. A small crowd had already gathered, the men and women who waited on the queen: handmaidens dressed in the finest garments that came through Musiri, the port just a few kilometres west of Vanchi; young men who fancied themselves poets and, more often than not, were in desperate throes of passion for the queen's handmaidens and the usual assortment of musicians, goldsmiths, merchants.

As the trio searched for a vantage point, Uthiyan found his way blocked by a corpulent, beringed gentleman – a jeweller, no doubt – fanning himself with the edge of his waistcloth, who had turned to whisper to the young man on his right, leaning against a frangipani tree, 'Why has the Perumdevi invited her?'

'The Perumdevi believes her husband is more interested in warfare and hence does too much to honour Kuttuvai. She believes that Agastya, even though his temple is here, has been slighted. So the Perumdevi hopes the descendant of the dancer Agastya once visited the heavens to watch will placate the angry sage.'

The jeweller shook his head. 'The queen has a good heart. A kind heart. She is immensely generous. But should she interfere in matters of state?'

The young man shrugged and turned back to watch the dance and, finally, Uthiyan had a clear view of the centre of the mandapam.

Of Madhavi.

The first thing he saw were her eyes, enormous and expressive. Only then did he take note of the rest of her – black hair swept up and coiled in an intricate style and artfully studded with jasmine flowers. She was exquisitely dressed. Her bodice was made of pearls fitted over her breasts and fastened with a gold mulaikaccu. A beautiful woven yellow cloth was wrapped around her legs and fastened at the flare of her hips by a megalai, a waistband of many gold strings and with little bells that chimed as she moved.

She was arresting but she was not what Uthiyan had expected. Even from the distance that he was at, there was the faint whisper of grey in her hair, the slight thickening of flesh at her navel. She was not as young nor as slender as any of the maidens that dotted the edges of the courtyard.

Then she began to move. And Uthiyan was lost.

For when she moved, it was as if her body was transformed into a statue of molten gold. Twisting and bending as naturally as a sunlit river flows down a mountain.

Not human, but something divine.

'At first I thought she was not so beautiful,' Shenguttuvan whispered to his brother and Sattan. 'But now, I confess, I think differently.'

'I thought the same too,' Sattan confessed, 'and I am at a loss to explain it. Where does her beauty lie? It is not in her face, nor in her form – there are other women who possess far more beautiful faces and forms.'

'In her clothing perhaps?' Shenguttuvan ventured. 'In the way she dresses herself?'

'That's part of it,' Sattan replied, 'but not all of it.'

'It is in her,' Uthiyan interjected for the first time, 'in the way she gives herself to her art.'

'Too much philosophy, brother!' Shenguttuvan shook his head. 'That answer is not for me.'

The music picked up tempo and Madhavi began to whirl. No longer a golden river, now she was a living flame, spinning in the sun-decked centre of the courtyard. It seemed as if her garments, her hair, her lustrous eyes had caught fire. A pillar of light, spinning to meet the heavens.

And then, cruelly – far too soon, it seemed to Uthiyan – it came to an end.

~

Sattan and Shenguttuvan lingered after the brief performance to do what young men do – attempt to flirt with the queen's handmaidens – but Uthiyan caught sight of a familiar figure, an old, gaunt man, leaving the grove.

'Paranar!' Uthiyan exclaimed in delight, running to catch up with him, as he stepped into the Silver Palace. 'What brings you here?'

'I came in the train of the Velir chief who arrived this morning.' The old man turned to greet the young prince as he pushed the door ahead of them open, to the queen's waiting room.

Seconds later the door swung open again and

the Perumdevi, Nalchonai, breezed in, dressed in an expensive purple Yavana cloth. Her hair, artfully dyed, was twisted up and fastened to the side and knotted with jasmine wreaths. A stunning necklace, made of strands of coral, pearls and gold, fell all the way to her waist. 'Paranar!' the queen exclaimed. 'Such a delight to see you again.'

Paranar bowed before the queen. 'It is an even greater pleasure to bask in the splendour of your company and the beauty of your incomparable city. But how are you, Perumdevi?'

'Oh Paranar! It has been such a trial since I saw you last. If I told you of the cares that I shoulder, mountains would weep.' The queen sighed theatrically.

'What ails the queen?'

'My husband doesn't care for me any more.'

Uthiyan sucked in his breath at his mother's response and darted a look at Paranar. The queen's issues with her husband were well known in court, but it was another thing to hear her discuss them so openly.

'Perumdevi, you have my sympathy. The burden borne by a queen is a heavy one,' Paranar replied glibly. 'Why, I have just come from the hills, from the court of Vel Pekan of the Aviyar, where the plight of his wife, Kannaki, tore our – mine and my friend

Kapilar's – hearts to shreds. For Pekan had become ensnared by the affections of a dancing girl.'

'A dancing girl? No, my problem with my husband is nothing like that. It is just that he doesn't listen to my council.' But Paranar's tactic had worked and this titbit of gossip had caught the queen's interest. 'But tell me more, what happened?'

'Oh, that poor woman, she has had a tough, tough time. And she asked Kapilar and me to intervene, to use our influence with her husband.'

'What did you do?' Now the queen was well and truly hooked.

'What influence do we have? What means did we have? The only thing at our disposal, our only means of persuasion, is our art. So Kapilar and I set to work with our songs, with our words, our poetry, on the stone-heart of Vel Pekan.'

'Did it work?'

'We wore him down eventually. We sang of the plight of his wife. We talked of her pain. We moved him by evoking the memory of his generosity, his goodness. In the end we prevailed. He abandoned the dancing girl and went back into the arms of his wife.'

'Your poetry has that sort of effect? It can shake a king's mind?'

'My lady' – Paranar was no longer glib – 'that is

what we do. That is the essence of our craft. We move in the homes of common folk and in the company of the highest of the land. We tell one of the other. It is part of our responsibility to tell kings, through our songs and stories, of what moves the hearts of common folk, of their griefs and sorrows, and it is our job to tell the common folk of the burdens and difficulties of kings. Our job is to present a point of view, an idea, an argument, a story that you may not have encountered before. We move hearts and through moving hearts we can change minds.'

'Paranar!' the queen, all excited, exclaimed. 'Move my husband's heart! Sing the song that you sang for Pekan to him!'

The old man bowed. 'I will endeavour to.'

There was a knock on the door. Shenguttuvan entered in the company of a messenger bearing the royal insignia of the Cheras, the bow and arrow. 'Uthiyan, our father bids us to attend on the Velir chief.'

'What's this?' the queen exclaimed.

Uthiyan cringed. 'Mother' – he rolled his eyes expressively towards Shenguttuvan – 'the betrothal.'

'Paranar,' the queen sighed, dramatically, 'you see how it is. No one tells me anything any more.' She turned to the messenger. 'Is my presence requested?'

Shenguttuvan, clearly uncomfortable, stared at the ground. The messenger fidgeted. 'No, Perumdevi. Only the princes.'

Uthiyan turned to look at his brother. Shenguttuvan was staring out of the window expressionlessly, but his fingers fussed with the dagger at his waist. Only Uthiyan knew that this meant the usually calm Shenguttuvan was nervous. His heart went out to his brother.

He reached out to touch Shenguttuvan's shoulder. 'Come, brother. Shall we?'

3

Shenguttuvan stared at his reflection uncertainly. Uthiyan, ignoring his elder brother's protests, had driven him back to their apartments and made him change into a fresh orange silk, and forced a set of gold katata on his arms, and around his neck one necklace of pearls and another one of gold and diamonds.

Uthiyan stood back, admiring his work, while Shenguttuvan fussed with the gold belt around his waist, adorned with the repeating motif of bow and arrow, the Chera symbols. 'It's not too grand?' the crown prince asked. 'Do you think she'll be able to actually see me under all this gold?'

Uthiyan let out a frustrated sigh. 'Trust me, brother, she'll like this. Poor princess, she has come a long way to see you. The least you can do is look the part.'

Shenguttuvan smiled and patted Uthiyan's cheek, as they made their way to the main hall. 'What would I do without you, dear brother?'

The pattimandapam was vast and studded with teak pillars, carved exquisitely by master craftsmen. Each pillar depicted a story or figure, part of the Chera lineage or history. Uthiyan took up his post, resting against a pillar extolling the exploits of his famous ancestor, his namesake, the first Uthiyan, founder of the Chera dynasty. Just ahead of him was the raised dais on which was mounted the Chera throne, gold-plated and studded with precious gems. Out of the back of the throne rose the head of a crocodile, carved out of wood and covered in gold leaf, facing upwards with its jaws parted as if it were about to consume its prey. It had egg-shaped rubies for eyes and pearls for teeth. The rest of the throne was fashioned in the shape of an elephant, its giant, life-size legs made of gold.

The hall was full, with many of the choice spots taken, and filled with a low buzz, for this event promised much excitement. The inner circle of the court, composed of the king's ministers, the priest of the war goddess Kuttuvai, the army chief, envoys and ambassadors, and the king's master of spies, were all present. So too were all the other cogs of the Chera court's machinery – accountants and treasurers, clerks, scribes and officials, the aristocrats and leading merchants of Vanchi and the chiefs of the army divisions. And last but not least, the palace guards and servants, at the very edge of the hall, along with the musicians, dancers and jesters who entertained the court. In fact, it seemed to Uthiyan that half of the combined population of Vanchi and Musiri had squeezed themselves into the hall. And the queen was not invited. Uthiyan's heart went out to his mother.

The brothers had arrived in the nick of time, for scarcely had they taken their positions when the heralds began to bang their drums to announce the arrival of the king. The ceremonial guards, archers bearing the bow and arrow, entered the hall, and after the archers came the king, Ko Nedum Cheralatan, followed by a company of the palace guards who stationed themselves in front of the throne. The king ascended the dais, and sat upon his throne, and Shenguttuvan weaved his way through the crowds, to take his post by the right side of the king, as was the custom for the heir to the throne, the Komahan.

The heralds banged their drums again, this time to announce the arrival of the Velir chief from Ilinji.

The Velir entourage was nothing to match the one

that had just come in, but Uthiyan was impressed nonetheless, for the Velir's bodyguards looked to be hand-picked, and although their clothes and garments were not much to boast of, it was clear, from the way they moved, and their well-muscled and battle-scarred frames, that these were men of considerable fighting experience.

The chief himself was far older than Uthiyan had imagined, and was brought in on a palanquin carried by four men.

'Old and weary,' a voice whispered into Uthiyan's ear, and the prince turned around to find Paranar next to him. 'But clinging to the chieftainship with the last ounce of strength left in his bones and all the guile he has acquired in six decades.'

The palanquin was followed by a girl, slightly younger than Uthiyan himself, her eyes demurely fixed to the floor.

'And that's the daughter,' Paranar added.

Uthiyan couldn't see much, until the palanquin stopped by him, in front of the throne. With the help of one of his men, the Velir chief descended from his litter. It required both the man and the chieftain's daughter to get the chief up on to the dais, and to the seat next to the king. When the chief had been seated, the girl looked up, a trifle hesitantly, at Shenguttuvan.

Uthiyan got a brief glance of doe-shaped eyes, a pleasantly pretty face and an intricate hairstyle made of numerous coils of hair and studded with pearls. But what impressed him far more was the alert curiosity in the glance that the princess gave Shenguttuvan. It was obvious that she was assessing the prince, and after a few moments, a sudden, shy smile sprang to her lips. Uthiyan exhaled, relieved. Clearly the princess found Shenguttuvan acceptable – and judging by the dazed look on his brother's face, Uthiyan was in no doubt that Shenguttuvan found his bride-to-be more than acceptable.

Paranar pinched Uthiyan's arm and gestured to the throne – where the king and the Velir chief were conversing, in low whispers. After a while, the king nodded. He turned to his eldest son and announced, 'The Velir chief tells me that before the betrothal, it would please him to have your horoscope cast.'

Shenguttuvan, somewhat nonplussed, assented, and then, another wizened, gaunt old man was brought forward. As he neared, Uthiyan observed that one of his eyes was almost entirely milky white.

'Who is he?' Uthiyan asked Paranar.

'The Perumkani, who happens to also be the

chief's younger brother. An astrologer and seer of great repute.'

The seer was brought to stand beside the Chieftain, who then spoke, confirming Paranar's words. 'This is my younger brother, my adviser. While I rule over men, he can read the omens of nature, and he understands the language of the stars and planets, and his counsel I always follow. For the fate of my daughter and this alliance I ask for his guidance.'

A courtier offered a stool, but this the seer declined, preferring instead to sit on the floor. Out of a cloth bag he pulled out a stack of old palm leaves. He motioned Shenguttuvan to sit before him, and in a low tone proceeded to ask him questions, as he sorted through the stacks of leaves.

'What is he doing?' Uthiyan asked Paranar.

'They say that on those palm leaves the entire future of this universe is written.'

'What do you mean?'

'Everything is destined. And everything that happens repeats over and over again. All is destroyed and recreated, and everything plays out exactly as has been written. Your future, mine, your brother's – everything is written on those leaves.'

Uthiyan frowned, sceptical, and glanced over at the stacks of leaves. 'He has just a few. There couldn't be more than a thousand leaves.'

'He has all that he needs to reveal the destiny of those he is fated to meet in this lifetime. That too is written, that too is ordained.'

'Do you believe all this?'

Paranar shrugged. 'He is very well reputed. And the Velir chief claims he has survived to rule for six decades with his help. There must be something to it.'

Now, the old man had narrowed down his selection to just two leaves. One was whole and the other was a much tattered fragment.

He asked Shenguttuvan a question and frowned. He picked up the whole leaf.

And his frown deepened.

'What is it?' the king asked, impatient.

The old man spoke. 'Does the prince have a brother?'

Bewildered, Shenguttuvan looked over at Uthiyan. 'Yes.'

'May he approach?'

The king nodded, a trifle warily, and Uthiyan ascended the dais.

The old man turned to Uthiyan. 'Is your mother different from his?'

Uthiyan, perplexed, nodded.

'Is she of the Cholas?'

Uthiyan nodded again.

The old man looked down again at the leaves in his hand.

The king, impatient, let out an exasperated sigh. 'What is this all about, old man? Come, now. We have been patient.'

The seer picked up the whole leaf and raised it. 'King, this leaf tells me Shenguttuvan's future. That the prince will grow to be a renowned warrior, command an army and make great conquests. That he shall live to a good age.' Then he set the leaf down and picked up the tattered fragment. 'But this other leaf – and there is only a fragment of it left, for much has been lost and destroyed in the great flood eleven years ago – tells me of your other son's fate. That he is born of two royal houses, ruled by the signs of the leaping tiger and the bow and arrow, and that he is the younger of two sons.'

The king gestured impatiently. 'Yes, we know that!'

'It also tells me that his name will be greater than that of his brother's, that his fame will eclipse that of his brother's, who will only be remembered through him, and that he shall outlive his brother.'

Uthiyan was stupefied. His jaw dropped. He looked over at his brother.

'What does this mean?' Shenguttuvan stuttered.

'The rest of the fragment is illegible or destroyed. This is all I can tell. I do not know what it means.'

'It is obvious,' the Velir chief snapped. 'It is the younger son who will one day be the Chera king.'

4

Chaos ensued. The king dismissed the court and strode out of the pattimandapam with his chief amaiccar, the principal minister, in tow. The air was thick with rumours circling, whispers buzzing, arguments reaching a fever pitch. Uthiyan felt dizzy. He was suddenly inexplicably weary, his head ached, his knees shook – and all he wanted to do was to lie down.

Uthiyan had noticed the courtiers glancing at him speculatively – all of whom had until now dismissed him as a dilettante younger son, someone who would one day be given a cushy position at court.

Uthiyan had counted on that too.

What could this mean? Uthiyan grabbed Paranar in the chaos. Could the astrologer be wrong?

'No,' Paranar had whispered, shaking his head.

'His skills as a fate teller are unsurpassed. He has never erred.'

Uthiyan snatched a look at his brother – Shenguttuvan's eyes were glazed, he was in a state of shock. Uthiyan grappled for words. He opened his mouth. Then shut it again.

The brothers stared at each other wordlessly.

'Komahan, Ilango,' a herald, panting, approached them. 'The king bids you to join him.'

The herald led them to one of the antechambers in the main palace, filled with maps of Chera territories and the surrounding Chola and Pandya lands. Dusty scrolls, with records of taxes and grants, lay stacked against one wall. With the king were the Velir chief, his brother and daughter, and the minister who was the king's chief adviser and the leader of the inner circle of the court, who was responsible for recommending the alliance.

'I have no desire,' the Velir chief was saying to the king, 'for my daughter to be a widow, and worse, to be a widow whose heirs will never inherit. I have raised her to be a queen. She will be an excellent one. And I am undertaking this alliance with you, in part to ensure that there is no war between us, and that alliance is sealed by the understanding that some day my grandchildren will be Chera monarchs, and ties of blood will bind the Cheras and Velir, not merely a wedding. You understand that.'

'What do you mean?' asked the king's councillor. 'Are you suggesting that this alliance that we have worked towards for years is off? Is that what you are saying?'

'No.' The chief shook his head. 'Wed my daughter to the other son.'

Uthiyan's jaw dropped. 'W-what?'

'Be silent,' the king snapped.

Uthiyan looked over at Shenguttuvan, who – for the first time in his life – was staring at him with barely concealed resentment.

And the princess, Venmal, too was looking at him, with a slight sense of distaste. 'Father,' she said, 'you can't just switch bridegrooms–'

'Yes,' the Velir chief replied, 'I can and I will. You are my daughter, and you have a duty and responsibility to the station of your birth. You will do what is decided.'

'Do you have so much faith in the word of your brother?' Shenguttuvan retorted sarcastically.

'Yes,' the chief replied simply. 'His counsel has never proven wrong.'

The king raised his hand. 'Enough. My other son has not been raised to be a king. I must think on this.

You will have my decision soon.' He rose and swept out of the chamber, followed by the Velir chief.

As Shenguttuvan turned to leave, Uthiyan pulled him back. 'Brother, I …'

Shenguttuvan cut him off. 'No,' he bit out, 'I have no wish to talk to you.'

Outside, Uthiyan fought his way through a melee of gossiping, obsequious courtiers. Where was Sattan? He needed to talk to his friend.

'Uthiyan!' a voice screeched. He turned around and caught sight of Sattan wading through the courtiers to reach him.

'Where is your brother?'

Uthiyan shook his head. 'He did not – does not – wish to talk to me, Sattan.'

Sattan frowned. 'He is your brother. You must talk to him before the court starts pitting you one against the other. He must realize that.'

Uthiyan shrugged.

Sattan looked around at the courtiers circling Uthiyan like vultures. 'Come, this is not the best place to talk. Even walls have ears here.'

5

They stopped by a pond, not far from the temple of the goddess Kuttuvai. Uthiyan, exhausted, sank to the ground, his knees giving way.

'And what about your father?' Sattan continued. 'Do you think he will heed the words of the fortune teller?'

'Perhaps.' Uthiyan buried his face in his hands. 'He wants this alliance. He might even stake his own sons to win it for his kingdom. Sometimes I think he sees us not as sons, but as pawns to be used and discarded.'

Sattan pursed his lips thoughtfully. 'So what do you think the fortune teller meant?'

'I do not know.'

'You are destined for something great – that's what he said.'

Those words. Something in Uthiyan, that he did not know he had, leapt at those words.

'A king!' Sattan exclaimed. 'Ko Uthiyan!'

Uthiyan felt uncomfortable. As if he was stealing something that was not his. 'Not so loud, Sattan!'

'But what if that was,' Sattan said in a whisper, 'what the fortune teller meant? King Uthiyan?'

Uthiyan could not fathom it. 'No.' He shook his head. 'The astrologer must be wrong.' He pulled himself up. 'Come, I must visit my mother.'

~

The queen had outdone herself in the preparations for the night's performance, but few turned out to hear Paranar's poetry. The events of the day had proved to be momentous and shocking, and Uthiyan suspected that the courtiers had, the moment the court had been dismissed, fled past the palace gates to break the news in the town. The queen, despite her position, had been the last to know – and when the news reached her, she had had a small pavilion erected in her courtyard and an invitation had been dispatched to the king. Her handmaidens and she had spent hours adorning the frangipani trees in her courtyard with oil lamps, twining garlands of jasmine around the pillars of the pavilions and erecting an artfully designed canopy of sky-blue silk, with pearls embroidered in the shape of the constellations, and arranging it exactly so that the sky above and its illusory twin below mirrored each other.

But all these clever, whimsical decorations, meant to please and gladden the king, were to no avail – for the Ko himself, at the last minute, sent a herald to tell the queen that he would not come. Neither did the Velir chief and his entourage. Uthiyan, too, with his ears still stinging from Shenguttuvan's rebuff, and his head in a whirl with the seer's prophecy, was loath to attend.

It was only when Uthiyan thought of his mother, alone in the midst of all the splendour she had put together, waiting for her husband, that he changed his mind. And when he arrived, he saw her downcast face light up.

'Uthiyan,' she exclaimed, raising one hand to caress his cheek. 'I always knew you were destined to be king.'

'No, mother,' Uthiyan replied, gently pushing her hand aside. 'The astrologer is wrong. It is my brother Shenguttuvan who is destined to be king.'

The Perumdevi pouted. 'But Uthiyan–'

'No.' He shook his head, resolute.

The Perumdevi had opened her mouth to argue further, but the performance began. And Uthiyan was glad, for Paranar's verses and music took his mind off the matters that plagued him and, besides, there was something else – Paranar had managed to persuade the dancer Madhavi to perform to his verses.

On the stage before him, beneath blue silk gleaming with pearls, Paranar strummed his old, seven-stringed yal, which had accompanied him as he journeyed across deserts, rivers, hills and forests, to entertain both kings and commoners. Beside him stood Madhavi – who was not dancing, but using expressive gestures to heighten the effect of Paranar's words. Uthiyan watched, fascinated, as Madhavi, with a slight tilt of her eyes, became a coquettish maiden, and then with the flare of her nostrils and widening of her eyes, a raging monarch. With a roguish smile and a flick of the wrist, she imitated, unmistakably, the poet himself, Paranar.

And now she transformed again, her arms spread forth in a gesture of entreaty, her eyes pleading, as Paranar sang his latest creation, the song he had composed to capture the plight of Kannaki, the abandoned wife of Vel Pekan.

How can you be so coldly cruel, so without
compassion?
As we were playing our small yals in the cevvali
raga of longing

and singing of your forest, the look of it during the
monsoon!
We saw a young woman in grief that seemed to
have no end,
her darkened eyes glowing like dusky, fragrant water
lilies but overflowing
with tears that fell to wet her breasts adorned with
their ornamentation
Bowing down to her, we asked of her, 'Young
woman! Are you some relation to the lord who
wants us to be with him?'
With her fingers like budding red kantal flowers
she brushed away her tears and then said to us,
'I am no relation of his!
Hear me out! Pekan, whose fame glows, hungers
for the beauty,
they say, of another woman who resembles me and
in his resounding
chariot he pays frequent visits
to the lovely city that is all encircled with jasmine!'

Paranar paused. Madhavi, arms outstretched, played the part of Pekan's wife, her brow furrowed, pleading, beseeching the poet.

The poet strummed his yal and moved across the stage. Uthiyan watched as Madhavi transformed with just a few gestures and a shift in posture from a heart-broken wife into a proud monarch.

Paranar sang again.

With your elephants in rut, with your proud horses, with your fame
that does not fade, Pekan, you who gave clothing to the dark
mindless peacock in compassion because it was shivering with the cold!
I come to you not because I am hungry, not because of the burden
of my family! But the gift for which I beg is that tonight
you may mount your chariot strung with bells and free her
of the anguish she lives with, and for that I sing – may those
who love mercy act with justice!

Uthiyan turned to see his mother wipe away a tear and glance at the empty seat beside her. There was no dancing girl, Uthiyan knew, and it would have been an easier matter had there been – the queen could have used her art, her beauty and her ploys to win her husband back.

History and politics were the queen's foes. For her brother, Uthiyan's uncle Karikala Chola, was the same monarch who had defeated Uthiyan's namesake, his grandfather, in battle. Unable to bear the shame of defeat, the old king had killed himself. And there were those who whispered that it was with a sense of bitter irony and revenge that the old king's son named his own child, nephew of his father's killer, after the first Uthiyan Cheral.

And the queen competed with a ghost, her predecessor, Shenguttuvan's long-dead mother, who through sheer imagining on the king's part had transformed into something she had never been in real life. She had been simple, quiet; a chieftain's daughter, and the king had mourned her when she died. Nalchonai was beautiful, fiery, wilful and sophisticated; it was a match of fire and water. Early on in the marriage, the king had reimagined his first wife into everything his second was not, a paragon of virtue, discrimination and temperament, but no more real than a dreamt-up phantom.

~

The next day the news sank in. Uthiyan woke to find the court a seething mass of rumours. Groups of courtiers speaking in hushed tones and breaking apart, guiltily, as he approached, as if they had just been speaking of him. Everywhere he turned, he heard his name being murmured. It seemed as if the very walls were conspiring against him.

And now the whispers seemed to gather and multiply into a roaring that filled his ears. Uthiyan sought to escape but at each turn he found someone blocking his path.

An army captain approached him and offered him an antique sword with a handle made of diamonds, said to have belonged to the first Pandyan king. Uthiyan mumbled an excuse and turned, only to encounter another courtier, begging to speak to him. This courtier, who Uthiyan had only before seen from a distance and never spoken to, proceeded to describe the charms of his unmarried, virginal daughter – her ample breasts, her reed-thin waist, so small that a hand would span it. In more hushed tones the courtier offered to loan this same daughter, for a night, if Uthiyan would promise to help in a dispute with his relative over property. When Uthiyan appeared unmoved, the courtier proceeded to speak of his handsome nephew.

Speeding away from him Uthiyan almost collided with a Yavana merchant with a crate of expensive wines, who looked delighted to see the prince – these wines, the merchant said, were intended for him. Uthiyan shook his head again, in a hurry to escape from the palace into the surrounding gardens, and to his mother.

There, in her Silver Palace, far removed from the court, he thought he would find some quiet, some solace, to still the roaring in his head – but no, this was not to be. For even here, Nalchonai, thwarted from occupying the place meant for her, sought to fill his mind with dreams of power. And he resisted, until she, his mother, who knew him so well, cast the one snare that would have him dancing to her tune.

'Just imagine,' the queen said, pacing the length of the room, 'just dream of the court you could create, the kingdom you could establish, the world you can build. Your brother and your father are alike – so preoccupied with the trivial matters of the court and the petty intrigues they engage in with other kings that they just can't see beyond, into the future.'

She stopped in front of him and jabbed a finger into his chest. 'You, *my* son, you can. They dream of wars and conquest and glory. Of brutality. Of tribute. But what do you dream of?'

Uthiyan shook his head. 'I do not dream of what is not mine.'

Nalchonai grabbed his hand and clutched it tightly. 'No! I know you and I dream of the same thing. A court, a kingdom, a world of beauty. Not of endless wars and conflicts. Just imagine what we could create. What a kingdom of beauty might be like. A city of the devas, here on earth. A world of harmony.'

Perhaps his mother was right, Uthiyan wondered. Was this his duty? Was this his destiny?

What kind of kingdom would he create?

One of great beauty, Uthiyan decided, of silver and golden palaces, and legions of dancing courtesans. One where he commanded an army of dancers and poets, not soldiers.

A world where kings, instead of going to war on battlefields, waged war through other means – battles of the mind fought with words – poets and philosophers debating the origins of the world and the forces that shaped man's actions and the hungers that moved the soul. A kingdom of ideas, poems, music and dance.

Could this be, as his mother insisted, the will of the gods?

~

His friends Sattan and Paranar found him hours later, spreadeagled on the sloping roof of the Silver Palace, gazing at the stars in an attempt to divine their language and his fate from their movements.

They too stared at the heavens, but nothing was revealed – for the stars were obscured by thunderclouds gathering at the edge of the horizon, preparing for a storm.

What was destined to be?

'There are rumours of a warmongering clan from up north,' Paranar told Uthiyan, repeating what he had heard on his journeys. 'Of men fierce and as hard as the stone found in those parched, barren lands. They have united to form a mighty army, tied by bonds – not of loyalty or kinship, but something else – a faith as immovable and hard as the stone-filled land they come from. The followers of Mahavira believe this will be the acme of the age of extreme sorrows, before the earth can ascend again. A time of great war.'

'War!' Sattan exclaimed, eyes agleam. Uthiyan knew that Sattan dreamt of war, of victory and coming home laden with spoils. Uthiyan himself had no taste for war nor blood. But war was what kings had to do.

And war, if Paranar was right, would soon be upon them. 'War,' he said, sighing heavily, 'I care not for war.'

Paranar turned to look at him. 'What do you care for then, Prince?'

Sattan chuckled. 'He cares for poetry! He fancies himself a poet.'

Paranar raised an eyebrow. 'Truly, Prince?'

Uthiyan shook his head. But Sattan wouldn't have any of it. 'He is a good one, too!'

'Prince, I would be honoured if you share your poetry with me.'

Uthiyan was too shy, too uncertain to share his efforts with Paranar. 'The poems are not very good.'

The old man smiled. 'Perhaps you judge yourself too harshly.'

Sattan nodded. 'That's exactly what I tell him.'

Uthiyan felt pressured. On the spur, he recited the lines that had come to him as he watched his mother dab her eyes, waiting for his father to arrive for the entertainment she had organized for him – listening to Paranar speak of another red-eyed queen and her estranged husband.

A girl, eyes reddened from her sleeplessness
holds in her hands a coral pestle.
She crushes white pearls in her little mortar

The greedy eyes of a girl crushing pearls
cannot be compared with innocent lilies
These red eyes are cruel.

He stopped, uncomfortable.

'It's good, isn't it?' Sattan exclaimed, loyally.

Paranar nodded slowly, but Uthiyan could not help feeling that he was pandering to him, a prince, son of one of his most powerful and wealthy patrons.

'It's not bad, Prince,' Paranar finally replied, cautiously, 'but it could be better.'

'How?'

'What is the woman doing? And how do you make the audience feel what she is feeling? That's what you have to do – so thoroughly create an image of the woman that she seems real to whoever listens to your poem, that your words conjure flesh and blood, colour, tears. When she cries, your audience too is moved to tears. When she feels joy, your words make your audience feel joy too.'

'How does he do that?' Sattan asked, curious.

Paranar paused. 'It is hard to teach that craft. But observe your own feelings. What moves you to joy? How does sorrow feel? How does it express itself? Understand the signs of these emotions and you will be able to describe them.'

Uthiyan inclined his head, considering Paranar's advice.

'But the most important thing about our poetry is the way the land and the soul merge,' Paranar added.

Sattan frowned, confused. 'What do you mean?'

'All art, all dance, all poetry and music seek to breach the boundary between the inner and the outer – between what is felt and what is seen, between the human and the divine, between the soul and the material forms of our world – making them one. If there is a song set on the seashore, it must always involve a long separation of lovers, since this is a place of parting. The outer world tells us the state of the inner feeling.'

Uthiyan sighed. This was too much to accomplish and digest. 'It's too much to do, Paranar.'

Paranar chuckled. 'Perhaps for a prince, yes. But this is what a poet must do to earn his living.'

'Poetry is for poets, then. Not for princes,' Uthiyan mused. 'What do poems matter to a prince when war is imminent?'

'Prince, sometimes, war can be averted with poems,' Paranar replied. 'Have you not heard of Avvaiyar, the poetess? When her best friend, King Athiyaman of Tagadur, sought to prevent war from breaking out with the Tondaiman of Kanci, he sent Avvaiyar as his envoy. Tondaiman took Avvaiyar to his armoury to show off his strength and send the message that he could defeat Athiyaman easily. And truly, his armoury was more impressive than the one at Tagadur.'

Uthiyan was transfixed. 'So what did she do?'

Paranar laughed. 'Avvaiyar scoffed and responded in verse. She told Tondaiman that though his armoury was well stocked and his weapons in perfect condition, Athiyaman was a far better warrior. And that his arsenal was severely depleted, stocked with only a few nicked and dented weapons, was true – because most of his weapons were under repair on account of being regularly used. In a nutshell she conveyed that Athiyaman was a superior combatant – he didn't merely display his weapons, he *used* them well.

Sattan was amused. 'And that prevented a war?'

'Yes.' Paranar smiled. 'That time it did. Until a prince from this palace, a Chera, went to war and came back with Athiyaman's head. That too is often the fate of kings.'

~

Later, the friends parted and Uthiyan took an indirect route back to the palace, one on which he hoped to avoid gossiping courtiers. As he made his way through the queen's pleasure gardens, he heard a woman utter a low-pitched groan.

He turned to find the source. Magically the clouds parted to reveal a full moon that illuminated a woman leaning against a tree, bending over to examine her raised ankle.

Hearing him approach, she looked up.

It was Madhavi.

6

Hours later Uthiyan tried in vain to figure out how it all happened. He knew he had knelt by Madhavi's feet, trying to identify the cause of her injury, which turned out to be a broken catch on her anklet that had pierced the tender skin of her ankle. He had prised out the hook. Then, he had torn a strip from his upper garment and used it to bind her foot. She was anxious that the hook would leave a cut, but he ascertained that it was a mere graze, not a wound. To be doubly careful, he had removed the offending anklet and knotted it into the free edge of his upper garment.

'It is rare to find a prince both so handsome and so solicitous,' the courtesan had commented.

Uthiyan blushed, and hoped that the darkness concealed his embarrassment. Apparently, it didn't, for Madhavi laughed softly. 'Oh Prince, men don't realize how enticing their softness is to a woman.'

Which only served to embarrass him even more.

'I heard today of what happened in the palace,' Madhavi said, breaking the silence. 'Of what the astrologer predicted. That you will be a great king some day.'

Uthiyan sighed. 'It seems a destiny that belongs to someone else, not me.'

'Why do you say that?'

'All my life I have been a second son. I love poetry, I love dance. I was indulged in these things, being a mere second son. If I must be a king, I have to suddenly change into a creature that I am not, and lose the things I love the most. I love my brother too, and I cannot but think that he would make a far better ruler than I could ever be.'

'We are often not what we imagine ourselves to be, Prince. The fact that you love all these things may in fact be what is destined to make you great.'

Uthiyan shifted uneasily. The conversation was getting uncomfortably personal. He tried to switch topic. 'Your performance last night was enthralling,' he said to the dancer.

'I will take that as an even greater compliment, Prince, for though Paranar and I are great friends, I did not much care for that poem of his.'

Uthiyan was surprised. 'Why?'

The palace was in sight, guards with torches posted around the perimeter. Madhavi stopped and turned to look up at him. 'He wrote about the woes of the wife. But did he ever care to consider the lot of the dancing girl? Prince, I remember what the plight of the dancing girl is – since I was one not so long ago. Now I am rich and famous, but once, in my youth, I was just one of many dancing girls, beautiful but with no money or fame to distinguish her. And then I met a patron, just like the dancing girl in Paranar's poem did, and he was married to another woman. So I know, I can imagine the other side of the story, the one that Paranar did not speak of.'

In the moonlight, Madhavi's eyes shimmered with unshed tears. Uthiyan wondered what a young Madhavi would have been like. Would a younger Madhavi have been innocent? Naive? Gullible?

And yet, it was this older version that had him captivated. The hint of deep sorrow that he had glimpsed beneath her sophisticated, worldly wise veneer fascinated him. Something in him stirred. He wanted to know more. More about her. More about her story and her sadness.

'What is that story?'

She sighed. 'Oh Prince, it happened so long ago,

but I imagine her story is not so different from mine. Although the man in question, a sea merchant, paid for my favours, I could not help falling in love with him. For he was a considerate lover, and generous – and something of a poet too. We spent delightful years together, and lived in luxury beyond imagining. Until one day, a ship of his did not return, and he lost everything he had. Then I found out that keeping me meant that he had borrowed beyond his means, and when his investment failed and the men aboard his ship did not return to their wives, he was ruined.'

There was a faint catch in her voice, but Uthiyan found it impossible to resist asking, 'What happened then?'

'I would have followed him into poverty, but no, he did not want me then. He went back to his wife, a good woman, a chaste one. He blamed me for what happened to him – it was the need for me that forced him to speculate rashly, he told me. And he did not want to see me or our child again.'

A tear now appeared at the corner of her eye. Uthiyan found himself wanting to wipe that tear, tracing its path with his eyes down the side of one lovely cheek, into the hollow of her neck, where it stopped. Madhavi exhaled deeply. The teardrop quivered. Uthiyan held his breath. She continued. 'At least I had a piece of him, I thought, our son, who looked so much like his father. But no, a year later, an infant still, he caught a fever and died. I was left with nothing – truly nothing. My heart broke. I could not eat, I could not sleep, I could not even drag myself to dance. I did not want to live.'

Uthiyan was riveted. 'How did you find the will to live?'

'The divine takes everything from you, until you have nothing left to give. It took my love, it took my child. I think it is in that moment, Prince, that when you long for an end to your heart's suffering, you discover the existence of your soul.'

She paused, and placed his hand there, right at his sternum, just below his heart. 'Here, this is where it lives. You are forced to surrender your will to the will of the soul, your life to destiny. I realized then that I dance not to gain riches or fame, but because it is the one thing that I can do. Even when my heart is breaking and filled with sorrow, still I find a reason to dance. I dance because I must. It is my nature.'

Uthiyan's hands itched to reach out towards her. To pull her close to him, to feel her nearness, to breathe in her scent, to taste the tears that were now streaming down her face.

Should he?

No, Uthiyan pulled himself together. The time was not right.

'There are many who call us dancing girls whores, who see us as demonesses who tempt men away from their faithful wives. Perhaps that is true for some, but there are many truths. The truth is this – we are all seekers, for the knowledge that makes us content with our lot, content with what we are, to make peace with the tragedies that befall all of us.'

She cast a searching glance at him. 'I see that in you too, Prince, that desire to know. To seek.'

Uthiyan's heart was pounding now. She held out her hand.

Uthiyan grabbed it.

Madhavi glanced towards the palace, towards the guards, and led him to a copse of trees nearby. There, safely concealed from prying eyes, she drew him close. He heard her breathing quicken, and tugged her bodice loose. As if in a fever, he touched her breasts. She lifted her face to kiss him, her mouth tasting of honey and cloves.

He traced the edge of her ear with a finger, and then slid his hand into her heavy, jasmine-wreathed hair. She slid her hands down his body, her palms leaving a trail of fire on his skin. He gasped as the tension gathered in him, coiling like a serpent, and she smiled. He felt a jolt, like thunderbolt racing through his spine.

And then it was as if a voice in his head screamed – no!

Uthiyan was stunned to find his hand reaching for hers and stilling it.

What was happening?

He wanted her, that he knew, his body desired her. But he found that he couldn't. Despite his mounting desire, the pulse beating through him like a drum, something in him resisted.

'You are more beautiful, you are all that I want . . .' he started and then stopped, unable to find the right words to express himself.

Something just didn't feel right.

She seemed to have read his thoughts, and to his surprise, without speaking, began to retie her bodice and straighten her clothes. She stepped away from him and started walking towards the palace.

Uthiyan felt terribly, impossibly alone.

'Wait!' he shouted after her.

She stopped and turned around. 'Oh Prince, who are you?'

'I don't know!'

'A prince takes what is offered to him,' Madhavi said softy. 'He seizes his fate, he does not question it. He cannot pause on the battlefield to weigh the cost of war or to look into the souls of those he kills. So when the chance to be a great king is given to one who is a prince, born of a line of great warriors, when a beautiful woman comes to him, scion of kings who have enjoyed the favours of goddesses, when a lovely princess is willing to marry him, son of two great royal houses, and still, he finds himself locked in battle with his soul – who is he then?'

She gazed up at the palace rising over them. 'Is he truly a prince, one born and raised to rule?'

7

Uthiyan struggled to keep his eyes open, as the two men before the dais bickered, bouncing accusations back and forth. The issue under discussion was the right to a coconut plantation, and Uthiyan thought that their dispute would be humorous if it wasn't so boring. It was past noon, and already a hundred cases like this had been heard by the king. How did his father do this month after month?

Uthiyan thought back to the morning, when he had been roused by one of the king's heralds hammering on his door. It was scarcely dawn, in fact, it was closer to night – for the sky was still speckled with stars, and a slight pink mist had begun to stain the horizon.

It was the Public Day, the one day a month when the common folk could approach the king himself, and not merely one of his officers or magistrates, for justice or to express a concern.

The king, Uthiyan was informed, desired his presence.

So Uthiyan, his head still heavy and throbbing, rubbed the sleep from his eyes, and dressed hastily before making his way down to the pattimandapam. As he rushed towards the audience hall, he collided with his elder brother.

Shenguttuvan glared at him and straightened the edge of his upper garment. Uthiyan bowed and allowed his brother the right of way.

As they approached the dais, their father, already seated on his gleaming throne, gestured Uthiyan to his right side, towards the seat usually reserved for the heir apparent.

Uthiyan, bewildered, shot a quick glance at his brother. Shenguttuvan's mouth was agape with astonishment. It settled in a grim line as he made his way to the other seat, to the king's left.

'Let it be clear,' the king announced to both his sons, and the small gathering of councillors, 'I am not making or announcing any decision today. Shenguttuvan is still my heir. But in light of the prophecy, I feel it is wise that we begin training

Uthiyan in the skills of kingship, for he has little knowledge of how to rule.'

He signalled to the herald. Trumpets blared, drums were struck and the massive wooden doors opened to the public.

Uthiyan started in astonishment. For although it was just a few minutes past sunrise, a line had already formed before the pattimandapam, snaking up and down the massive steps, and across the length of the palace grounds. 'How long have they been waiting?' Uthiyan murmured aloud.

'Many of them waited through the night,' the king replied.

As the first petitioner stepped forth, Uthiyan turned to the councillor standing next to him.

'Can the king hear so many cases in one day?

'He tries,' the councillor replied.

The first case was an old woman demanding compensation from the king for the loss of her goats, who had been butchered by passing soldiers. Then, a deputation from the Nasrani, those who followed the teachings of a Yavana priest, petitioning for land to build a temple. An old man, who had lost his son in the last war, wanted to know who would perform the last rites. Representatives of two far-flung villages squabbling over the rights to the road to the nearest town, approached the king to decide the matter.

And so it went on and on and on. His eyes fastened on a young woman, further down in the line, listless and tired. Her eyes were red-rimmed, a figure who was the very incarnation of the woman from Paranar's poem the night before. What was her story?

In his mind, a poem began to form, the story of a young woman, seperated from her husband, grieving and now, with no support or help, seeking the king's justice.

'Prince!' a voice by his ear hissed. Uthiyan was jolted back to reality from his daydream, to discover that the councillor was tugging at his upper garment. The king, eyebrows raised, glanced peremptorily at his son.

The bickering pair, who Uthiyan recalled squabbling over coconuts, were making their way out, and now a curious knot of men made their way to the foot of the dais. As they approached, Uthiyan observed his father stiffen. They led a limping figure bound in chains.

'Antuvan,' the king whispered.

The chained man came closer, and Uthiyan noticed a shock of white hair and then the greyish stubble on a leathery face – and a strangely familiar scar that ran across one side of the man's face from just below his eye to the edge of his mouth.

Who was this?

'The king's former bodyguard,' the councillor replied, as if reading his thoughts.

And then Uthiyan recalled a younger man with black hair and a less battered face. And the story of the scar – how this man, Antuvan, had, in the famous battle with Karikala Chola, taken a blow that was intended for the king and thus saved his life.

But that man – young and smiling, with a laugh or jest always on the tip of his tongue – bore no resemblance to this maimed and bound figure in front of him.

'Antuvan,' the king said again, as if to himself. 'What happened to you?'

At the king's words, the man raised his face and Uthiyan noticed the king recoil, as if struck.

For the expression in his eyes was full of venom. Was it hate?

Or was it pain?

Over the next half-hour the full story emerged. Antuvan had been sent to command an expedition against a cattle-raiding tribe from the northern forests. But the mountainous terrain had proven treacherous, and the wily tribe, with their hideouts in the forest, sure-footed among the winding, stony mountain paths, had demolished their supply lines and sent a good number of Antuvan's men to their deaths.

Perhaps that had broken him, or perhaps it had been pride – for Antuvan, with his diminished troop, a famous war hero, who had once saved the life of the Ko himself, now had to accept a lower command in the next foray.

Clashes with his commanding officer were frequent. Finally, one morning, the camp awoke to the news that the commander was found in his tent, throat slashed.

All fingers were pointed at Antuvan, who was known to have differences with the commander. And the discovery of a scrap of cloth, clutched tightly in the commander's fist, that perfectly matched a piece missing from Antuvan's garment, had confirmed these suspicions.

'Some say that Antuvan had visited the shrine of one of the spirit-demons of the people who lived the forest. And that their priest had initiated him into the rites that would bring the demon-spirit into his body, so that he would be invincible in battle. After that day, Antuvan scoured the hills for prey – he single-handedly destroyed an enemy host, as if to avenge the lives of the men he had lost,' one of the men guarding Antuvan offered.

'And yet others claim,' said another, 'that it was to a girl from this tribe that Antuvan had lost his heart, and it was her wiles and tricks that had persuaded him to kill his commander.'

The king looked at his former bodyguard. 'Is this true?'

The man raised his head. 'No!'

The first man spoke again. 'Some say the demon began to possess him more and more, riding him like a deva rides his vahana, and soon all that remained of Antuvan was his skin.'

'No!' Antuvan shouted again.

'Then what is the truth?' the king asked.

Antuvan was silent.

'And yet he will not say what the truth is.' The soldier shrugged. 'He killed a man, his commander. The military tribunal sentenced him to death, but he appealed for the king's justice. What is to be his fate, Ko?'

The king sighed wearily. 'This man saved my life once. I find it hard to pass judgement because of this and many other reasons.' He turned towards Uthiyan. 'What say you?'

Uthiyan, surprised, almost fell off his seat. His head was in a whirl. Hitherto, all the judgements and issues had been harmless – disputes over property, compensation, arbitration – nothing that involved life and death.

Until now. This was real.

What was he to do? He knew that mutiny – which was what Antuvan was guilty of – was punishable by death. Though Antuvan had saved his father's life. He was a hero.

But he had killed his commanding officer.

Uthiyan took a look at the man in front of him. Battered, injured, his eyes spewing venom.

Was it possible that he was possessed by a demon?

How could a man be saved from a demon? Or had the demon taken over him entirely?

'What do you say, Ilango Uthiyan?' the king repeated.

Uthiyan wanted to ask for more time, but the line before the throne shifted and murmured and seemed to surge like a wave breaking on the shore. There was no time.

There were so many others waiting for the king's justice.

'The answer is obvious, Prince,' the councillor beside him whispered, trying to help.

Uthiyan gestured him to be silent. And thought again. He tried to think like a king would. What would a king do? A king would consider the crime and the just punishment. He would also take into account the consequences of his judgement – and in this case, a merciful judgement might send the wrong message to the commanders in the king's army. If mutiny was forgivable, could a commander rely on his men to be obedient, even during the heat and chaos of a battle?

Would mercy destroy morale?

'Execution.' Uthiyan managed the dreaded word out, but even to him it sounded like a whimper.

The king nodded and turned to Shenguttuvan. 'What say you?'

Shenguttuvan did not pause to think. 'Execute him, Ko.'

8

The day drew to a close. The lines of petitioners outside the pattimandapam dwindled and vanished, and night began to encroach upon the day. Uthiyan returned to his quarters, exhausted.

On a stool beside his bed lay Madhavi's anklet, the clasp still awry. He had forgotten to hand it back to her the previous night, in his confusion. Now that was another thing to be dealt with. He had to return it to her. How? Discretion was required, with everything else going on; another scandalous rumour, was the last thing he needed, especially when a marriage alliance with the Velir could be the cost.

Asking a palace servant to return it was out of the question – Uthiyan had better do it himself, he thought despite the embarrassment that encountering Madhavi again might occasion. And so, hooking the anklet into his garment, he set off for the palace guest house, where Madhavi was staying.

Uthiyan found that his thoughts, in spite of his best attempts to steer them in another direction, kept going back, insistently, to Antuvan.

Had he done the right thing?

His brother too had arrived at the same decision.

What troubled Uthiyan was that the king had decreed that in a week's time a scaffold be erected in the inner courtyard of the palace, which was used as a training ground for his personal troops. There, as was the custom, the mutineer Antuvan would be executed before the entire army. The man to swing the sword that would cleave Antuvan's neck from his body would be the prince who had first pronounced the judgement – Uthiyan. It was one thing to reach a just decision, the king had asserted, but entirely another to carry out justice. There was a difference between thinking justice and doing justice, and the king meant for his son to learn it.

Uthiyan had, over the hours, as the rest of the petitioners were dealt with by the king, imagined the execution day in great detail. Already, in his mind's eye, he could see the stage, and Antuvan, his head bent and neck bared. And Uthiyan, the king's great sword clasped in his hand, Uthiyan who never killed a man before, who had never been sent to battle, protected by his mother's protestations that her son was too delicate and gentle to face the horrors of war.

What would it be like? How many tries would it take to sever the a man's head from his body? He had heard that sometimes it was clumsy – not a swift, clean kill – that one had to hack and slice through muscle and tendon and bone.

What if, Uthiyan wondered, Antuvan was innocent? Could he truly be guilty if it was a demon that had driven him to kill? Was the man innocent if the demon was guilty?

What made one kind of murder more legitimate than the other? What made Antuvan a sinner and Uthiyan, his executioner, just?

These thoughts buzzed, swarmed, circled and chased each other in his head.

Uthiyan shook himself.

And found that his mind, engulfed as it was, had failed to direct his feet on the right path. For he was not outside the guest house, where Madhavi was, but his feet had conspired against him and led him to where the source of his anxieties was being housed: the prison by the barracks.

Uthiyan wavered for a few moments. But then his conscience intruded, and he found himself inside the barracks, bidding the guard on duty to take him to Antuvan's cell.

The cell was small and scarcely large enough for a man to lie down. Two men could barely stand there, and the guard was clearly uncomfortable at the thought of the prince entering this small cell.

Uthiyan took in the sight and smell of the cell – the grimy walls, the nasty stink. Is this how prisoners were treated? He looked at Antuvan, as bedraggled and unwashed as the cell, his hands and feet bound with a thick rope. But still, despite his maimed and broken state, there was dignity in him.

'What brings you here, Ilango?' Antuvan spoke first, breaking the silence.

'I have come because I wonder if I have done the right thing.' It felt like a relief to confess it.

'Ah. The prince wonders. He has a conscience.' There was a trace of a sneer in Antuvan's voice.

Uthiyan winced to hear it.

'I am to die in a few days, Prince,' the man continued. 'By your hand. I accept my fate. Can it be that you do not accept yours?'

'Do not speak to the prince that way!' The jailer, incensed, lunged at Antuvan.

Uthiyan held him back. 'Leave us.' The guard seemed eager to dispute this, but Uthiyan summoned every inch of royal training, and drawing himself to his full height, repeated imperiously, 'Leave us!'

The guard obeyed.

Antuvan clapped slowly from his corner. 'Oh, you do that well, Ilango.'

'I did not do it for your amusement,' Uthiyan spat out. 'I come to ask you a question that I do not think any prince has ever put to a man condemned to death. Before you die I give you one last chance to tell your side of the story. Is there anything that could justify your actions?'

'There is. Do you care to hear it?'

'Yes.'

'The man I killed, the commanding officer, he was a brute. With unnatural tastes. We captured a young man, a boy, really, during a skirmish. The commander took him for his own, bound the boy to his tent pole with a chain. The commander relished punishment, I could see it in him, that he enjoyed humiliating others. He found a sick, depraved pleasure in it. Not merely beating them, not merely the sight and smell of blood. But the cries for mercy, for help, just spurred him to inflict more pain. To use words to wound. He treated the boy like an animal, feeding him just like one would feed a dog. I saw the boy, with bruises and cuts. Broken bones that would never mend properly. Broken not merely in body, but in spirit too. Death would have been kinder. And one day, the boy could no longer take it. He tried to run away.'

Antuvan took a deep breath before continuing. 'But of course they found him and brought him back. And the commander, to punish him, cut off his tongue. Not long after, the boy tried to escape once again. Can you imagine how terrible it must have been?'

He shut his eyes, as if in pain. 'And this time, he cut off other things. I heard that boy howling in the night, his tongue mangled, like a dog. I went into his tent and found the commander watching the boy bleed to his death, slowly, on the floor. He was drinking expensive Yavana wine in a fine glass – and watching this boy die.' Antuvan looked up at Uthiyan. 'There is only so much a man can take. I saw the eyes of that mute, dying boy, his eyes, turned towards me, begging. What would you do in that situation, Prince?'

Uthiyan felt sick to his stomach. He shook his head. 'I don't know.'

'I did what I thought was right. No one should die that way. And so I drew out my dagger and slit the boy's throat. Right there. A quick end. The commander was furious. He threw the wine in my face. I had just spoilt his entertainment, I was told. He then slapped me.'

Antuvan paused. 'And I killed him, before I even knew what I was doing. Oh, I heard those men today. They said it was the work of a demon or a spirit. No, Prince, it was me. And I would do it again.'

'Why did they lie? Why is your story different from theirs?'

'They did not lie, Prince, they told you what they chose to see. They chose to be blind to the commander's evil. They chose instead to talk of rules and order and discipline and hierarchy. The army is nothing without those. They might well be right.'

Uthiyan grimaced. 'Why did you not tell my father? He would have believed you.'

Antuvan shrugged. 'There are other things I have seen, Prince. Ugly things. Things that would give you nightmares and make your skin crawl. That is what war does. It brings out the ugly, dark side of men. If I told the king what all I knew, I think his head would fall from his shoulders. After all the goddess that he worships, whose service he is pledged to and whose shrine stands on the palace grounds, is Kuttuvai, the goddess of war.'

'But you must tell him!'

'Why, Prince? A kingdom depends on conquest,

on safe borders. I have argued this to myself, I have found many reasons.'

There was no way he could execute this man. 'I cannot kill you,' he said.

'What is your other choice? Will you expose this story and shame the army, the very soldiers who have fought so loyally for your father? If you go to the king, he will tell you that questioning the integrity of the army is something no king can do if he hopes to still rule the next day.'

What were his choices? If he couldn't execute him, if he couldn't approach the king . . . what else could he do?

'Could you escape?'

Antuvan considered this. He gestured to his bound hands and feet. 'I know this prison well, unlike the other prisoners here, I have guarded it many times. I know the ins and outs, the secret passages. The guard here, he is no match for me, even with a weapon. But what will I do, Prince, if I escape?'

'Go to another place. Start a new life.'

'No,' Antuvan replied. 'I do not know if I have the will to start a new life.'

Uthiyan, frustrated, paced the small chamber. Anger shot through him. His voice rose as he swivelled to face Antuvan. 'Are you prepared to die then?'

'No man ever is.'

'But you will die, by my hand, if you do not try to escape. Do you see any other way out of this?'

'And if I die trying, what then, Ilango?'

Uthiyan sighed. 'At least then it is not on my head.'

'Prince, you are an honest man.' Antuvan said to Uthiyan. 'That is rare.' He nodded. 'I shall try.'

Uthiyan rapped sharply on the prison door.

In a trice, the jailor appeared. 'Prince?'

'I need to question the prisoner. He is refusing to answer me. I need instruments that will make him talk.'

The guard bowed, and pulling the door shut, escorted Uthiyan to another room in the same premises.

He looked around. There was a pincer, hanging from a nail on one wall, that Uthiyan knew was used to extract teeth, nails and even organs. A knuckle duster in another corner, beside a selection of knives. Baskets, stacked against the wall that Uthiyan knew, were filled with parasites that could be applied to open wounds. A pierced sphere attached to a handle, by which burning oil could be poured on to a prisoner's skin.

'Bring me the pincer.' The guard hurried to do his bidding. Uthiyan slipped a small, sharp knife into the folds of his clothing when the guard had turned away. It looked like an ordinary knife, something easily missable that could not be traced back to him or this place. Antuvan could use it to hack through the cords binding his hands and feet.

As the guard brought the pincer to him, Uthiyan waved it aside dismissively. 'I've changed my mind. Leave that.'

'Prince?'

He picked up the knuckle duster. 'I will use this. Take me back to the prisoner.' He swept regally out of the chamber, trying his best to act imperious.

The guard shot him a confused glance, but hastened to follow the order. In minutes, Uthiyan was back in Antuvan's cell.

'Leave us.'

The guard made as if to protest, but Uthiyan raised his hand. The guard shut the door again.

Uthiyan shivered. The guard seemed the sort that relished torture. What did they do to prisoners here? There was not time to contemplate that, though. He had to pull himself together.

'Here.' Uthiyan brought the knife out and tossed it beside Antuvan. 'Hide it. But you cannot leave it here, or use it on the guard. They cannot trace it back to me.'

Uthiyan's eyes fell on the anklet fastened to his upper garment. He hesitated and then untied it. It seemed to him that Madhavi, renowned dancer that she was, would have innumerable anklets – his mother had a set for every day of the week. There were no etchings or gems to suggest that it was more than an ordinary anklet, but it was heavy and would fetch a good price. Madhavi hadn't even noticed this one was missing. It probably meant nothing to her. 'Here,' he said, and tucked it inside Antuvan's clothing. 'Take this. You might need it after your escape.'

Antuvan bowed. 'You are a good man, Ilango. You will make a good king.'

9

Cries sounded in the night. Uthiyan awoke and crossed over to the window overlooking the inner courtyard. Lifting the blinds, he saw soldiers swarming in the courtyard and the resident commander screaming orders, while the palace attendants lit torches and handed them to the soldiers.

Uthiyan dressed hurriedly and rushed to the courtyard, where he found Sattan. 'Can you believe it?' His friend whispered excitedly, 'The prisoner, the one you sentenced, just escaped.'

Uthiyan had expected this. As he watched, the guard, the same jailer who had led him to Antuvan, was brought into the courtyard, limping. He also had a split lip and a bruised eye, as if he had been in a fight. As he was being treated, Uthiyan saw the commander exchange words with him. They turned to look at Uthiyan.

Uthiyan could guess what was going to happen next. The commander approached him.

'Ilango, may I ask you a few questions?'

Uthiyan nodded assent.

'The prison guard says that you are the last person to have visited Antuvan.'

'Was I? I must be if he says so.'

The commander shifted uncomfortably. 'May I ask what took you to visit the prisoner?'

Uthiyan had his answer prepared. 'It is simple, Commander. I have never killed a man before, even in the name of justice. I felt that if I must swing the sword that will deliver the death blow, I must also be prepared to look the man in the eye. I must question him to be sure that he tells me the truth, to know that my actions are just. I felt my father would approve.'

The commander relieved, retreated. It could be no comfortable task, Uthiyan imagined, to question a prince. He exhaled a pent-up sigh of relief.

Sattan sounded a low whistle. 'I never thought I'd see the day, finally, my friend Uthiyan has begun to behave like a prince and less like a palace low-life.'

Uthiyan smiled. 'I've not entirely left my low-life ways behind. Do you think there'll be any chance to sleep?

'Fancy a flagon of wine? My father got it off a

Yavana merchant and left it with me to ease the strain of being a clerk at the court.'

Uthiyan beamed. 'Spirits to keep the spirit up? I like the sound of that,' he chuckled.

~

After retrieving the flask from the dormitory where Sattan was housed with the other court clerks, the two young men set off in search of their secret getaway – the broken remains of an ancient pavilion behind the shrine of the goddess Kuttuvai.

As Sattan struggled to unstopper the flask, he asked, 'What's it like now? Being almost Komahan.'

'It's all changing so fast.' Uthiyan groaned and, sitting down, covered his eyes. 'Everything. I never imagined this would happen to me. I do not know, Sattan, if I am meant to be a king.'

'I can't imagine that your brother is too happy about it,' Sattan said.

'No,' Uthiyan agreed. 'He refuses to speak to me. The worst is this, Sattan, to keep wondering about the astrologer's prediction. Why would I make a better king? I keep thinking of Shenguttuvan – measuring his flaws and shortcomings. Forgetting to see the good side of him. Seeing him not as a brother, but as an enemy, a rival. That is the worst. And I have to wonder why my father listens to this astrologer, who is not even his astrologer, but merely one to a trumped-up petty chieftain who calls himself king.'

Sattan took a swig from the flask and handed it to Uthiyan. 'Hmm. I wonder if this could be some Velir game, a ploy to play brothers off against each other and start a civil war.'

'You think so?'

Sattan shrugged. 'It is possible, and I wonder if your father's strategy is actually to buy time.'

'I don't know.' Uthiyan sighed, and quaffed a large portion of the flask's contents. 'I wish this wasn't happening.'

'That defeatist attitude does not become a potential crown prince!' Sattan stood up and stretched himself. 'Come now, are you drunk as yet?'

'Almost.' Uthiyan grabbed the flask again and downed its contents.

'I'm impressed, Prince.' Sattan bent over in a mock bow. 'Why, this recent rise in your status has led to a proportionate rise in your ability to imbibe the finest Yavana wine. The sailors of Musiri would be most impressed.'

Uthiyan chuckled.

'When you are Komahan, and later, when you are

Ko, you musn't forget your friend Sattan. You must promise me now that you will appoint me as court clown. It will be a new post, and the Chera court will be much envied by the Cholas and Pandyas. Why, I will be known as the best court clown in all the three kingdoms, and my buffoonery, renowned in the whole of Tamilaham, will be the jewel in your crown, greater than the Sangam of Madurai. We shall have the Sangam of Vanchi, where I shall assemble the greatest buffoons and fools of Tamilaham, and the Chera court will be known for its crude, loutish humour, and the sailors of Musiri will carry our fame and our buffoonery to foreign shores! The Cholas and the Pandyas will vie to secure the second best clown for their courts, but none will be as great a jester as I!'

Uthiyan dissolved into laughter. 'And I shall go down in history as the Ko of the clowns!'

'Come on, dear Komahan, it's almost dawn, let's get up to some mischief and serenade the luscious Madhavi. And if that doesn't cause enough of a scandal to discredit your potential as a Komahan, we'll think of some other rowdy scheme.' Sattan pulled Uthiyan to his feet, and Uthiyan allowed himself, tipsy and drunk, to be led in the direction of the guest house.

They arrived there a good hour later, for Sattan stopped on the way to serenade a coconut tree, in rehearsal for serenading Madhavi, and Uthiyan – not to be outdone – decided to compose a poem to a shimmering red lotus they spied floating atop a small pond.

Finally they arrived – considerably after daybreak – to find the guest house a scene of a maelstrom. In the centre courtyard stood Madhavi, hair unbound and face grim, brandishing a stick of kohl as if it was a weapon of war, while a coterie of palace attendants cowered in fear before her.

Uthiyan and Sattan found Paranar, watching with barely concealed amusement, resting against one of the pillars of the courtyard.

'What's happening?' Sattan asked him.

'The famous dancer is throwing a tantrum,' Paranar replied, smirking. 'Today is the day of the festival of Indra, where she is to perform at the temple by the seashore, and she discovered that one of her anklets is missing.'

Uthiyan's heart stopped. 'Missing?'

Paranar nodded.

'But what is the problem with that?' Uthiyan tried to sound nonchalant. 'She must have half a dozen, a famous dancer like her, one for every day of the month!'

'This one was a special one apparently,' the old poet answered. 'A gift from Karikala Chola, who had these anklets specially made for her, filled with precious stones that he brought from his much famed expedition to the Himalayas. He gifted the pair to Madhavi after her arangetram, after which – and due to the anklets – Madhavi, the Chola king and the town of Puhar hold that the kingdom was blessed with rains after years of drought.'

'Sounds like a ton of nonsense,' Sattan replied. Still drunk, he reeled forward. 'I have half a mind to tell her that after I serenade her.'

'No.' Uthiyan, his senses returning, a queasy feeling in his gut, shook his head. Clearly Madhavi had forgotten that it was him who had taken her anklet the previous night, thankfully. But he had better leave before she remembered.

If it was discovered that he anklet had been with him and he had given it to Antuvan to aid his escape . . . Uthiyan's mind froze. Panic seized him.

'I think we should leave,' he told Paranar. 'Come, Sattan!' He yanked his friend and set off towards the exit.

'Wait,' Sattan mumbled. 'What about my song and your poem?'

'We'll do that another time!' Uthiyan almost shouted at him.

They had reached the doorway. As Uthiyan struggled to pull the half-reluctant, intoxicated Sattan through the door, he collided with a bulky form. He fell, and gazed up to look into the disdainful eyes of his brother.

Shenguttuvan gave him a look of disgust, straightened his clothes, and marched forward without a word.

Uthiyan was surprised. 'What brings my brother here?'

'Oh,' Sattan muttered. 'He comes here every day to make eyes at the Velir chief's daughter, Ilango Venmal.'

~

Hours later, a haze of heat lifted, scorching from the earth, rippling the air. The afternoon sun, in the brutal days before the onset of the much awaited monsoon, was savage. The sweat stung Uthiyan's skin, and his brain felt as if it was being pickled. The last few sleepless nights, the chaotic mess of the past week, the panic that still gripped him, from the news of Antuvan's escape and Madhavi's missing anklet, the ill-advised drinking spree with Sattan this morning

– everything seemed to combust together in the heat, into one pounding headache.

To add to that, he was seated up high on a wooden pavilion fixed to an elephant's back, in a procession just behind the Ko, an honour usually reserved for the crown prince. But the Ko, still playing strategy, had determined that this year both princes would share the same seat, and so Uthiyan found himself sitting next to a steely-eyed, gruff Shenguttuvan, as the procession wound its way through the streets of Vanchi and then through Musiri to the temple of Agastya by the shore, where Madhavi would perform the ritual invocation.

The silence hung between them, burning as fiercely as the noonday sun.

Uthiyan, uncomfortable, fussed with the brocaded edge of his silken upper garment. Finally, he could take it no longer. 'It's a hot day–'

'Why were you at the royal guest house this morning?' Shenguttuvan bit out before Uthiyan could finish.

Taken aback, Uthiyan floundered. 'I-I was there to see Madhavi . . .'

'Don't dare lie to me, little brother.' Shenguttuvan whipped around to face his brother, eyes blazing. 'You were there to see the princess!'

'No,' Uthiyan stammered, realizing that Shenguttuvan now saw him as a rival for the princess's affections. 'No, brother, I promise you–'

'You can have the cursed throne, the crown, the kingship – I care not a whit for all that!' Shenguttuvan roared.

'I don't want it–' Uthiyan tried to interrupt, all the while aware that they had captured the attention of the mahout, who was listening to this quarrel with great fascination.

'Take it and do what you like with it. Squander the treasury on your mother's expensive tastes. Empty out the granary feeding every poet and singer in existence in Tamilaham. Run the kingdom to the ground. Fill it with clowns and buffoons like you and your friend Sattan. But why must you have her too?'

'I don't want to marry–'

'Don't lie to me, brother!' Shenguttuvan twisted again in his seat to glare at Uthiyan. 'I saw you this morning.' He was close to tears. 'I thought my younger brother is a gentle sort. He still has to grow up but he is not a bad man. Perhaps he will make a better husband than I will. But then I smelt you – and you were stinking of that foul Yavana liquor! What sort of man goes to court a sweet, beautiful princess drunk? What sort of husband will you be? What sort of king will you be?'

10

The procession took hours, winding through the streets of merchants, charioteers, physicians and astrologers that surrounded the palace. And then through the quarter of the dancers, musicians and courtesans, and then back up through the suburbs where the army was stationed. From Vanchi it went across the river into Musiri and the suburbs of the fishermen, and through the harbour with its great warehouses and the fluttering masts of ships, and then the streets of fine houses occupied by the wealthy seafaring Yavana and Chera merchants who traded on the seas. Around the marketplaces and the streets where courtesans, jewellers, scent merchants, washermen and tailors lived, and past the suburbs where the Nasiri had been given space to build their church. Having done this hours-long circuit of the two towns, the procession moved back into Musiri, to where the temple of Agastya stood by the sea.

A stage had been set up by the temple. As ceremony dictated, Madhavi bathed and garlanded the talaikkol, the staff of the ceremonial white umbrella that shaded the Ko in battle and during ceremonial occasions.

Made of bamboo, this staff was embellished with gold and precious gems. Legend had it that after the sage Agastya had finished composing the *Tolkappiyam*, he sought a respite by visiting the court of Indra, the king of the devas. Indra wanted to please the illustrious rishi with a dance performance by the famed apsara Urvashi. But as Urvashi danced, she caught sight of the handsome Jayanta, son of Indra, and fell in love at first glance. Flustered, she missed a step.

Furious, the sage Agastya cursed her and Jayanta both to be born on earth and live out their earthly lives seperately, but later, witnessing the agony of these lovers and his anger cooling, he gentled his curse – Urvashi would be reborn as a dancing girl in Kanchi, and Jayanta, her lover, as a stalk of bamboo. The lovers would meet whenever Urvashi danced onstage. That is why a bamboo stalk, the king's ceremonial badge of office, was placed on the stage

– so that these lovers could meet, in spirit, and the dancer, invoking the spirit of Urvashi, danced for the eyes of the lover, hoping to please him with the excellence of her performance.

And so the Perumdevi, hankering after fame that would rival the Sangam, the gathering of poets that came together in the grand pattimandapam of the Pandyan king Neduncheliyan in Madurai, and the glittering court that graced her brother's reign in Kaveripattinam, had sought to invite Madhavi, the descendant of Urvashi herself, here to appease the sage who had cursed her ancestress.

As Madhavi ascended the stage, Uthiyan thought of all this, all those petty rivalries between kings, between poets, between dancers and poets, between commanders and their subordinates, between merchants, between kings and queens, between brothers. What did it all mean? What was the point of it?

A moment later, Madhavi's performance began, and all thoughts of dharma and kingship ceased, as Uthiyan watched, enraptured.

She spun, as if lighter than gossamer, and the very elements seemed to exist to adorn her performance. The ocean waves sparkled, glinting, and Madhavi appeared at times to be suspended, borne by the sea breeze, in the very air, between a sky the colour of coral and an ocean shimmering like a star-laden night – the glow of the setting sun transmuting her into a spinning, twirling, red-gold flame.

What lent even greater beauty to Madhavi's movements was that vulnerability, that loss, that sorrow – her story – that still clothed her features, veiled her glance. The slow, inexorable creep of age that marked her face and figure made one realize that this beauty was only of this moment, to be enjoyed now.

Uthiyan shivered, thinking of how a few nights ago this fleeting beauty had been within his grasp. Somehow, to his surprise, it was this – this matureness, the mixture of beauty and wisdom – that made him want her all the more. A feeling that grew stronger the more he saw her.

Was this love?

Something in him ached, as he watched her, hoping that her dance would not end.

Arms raised up to entreat the heavens, Madhavi spun, face turned to the sun, pleading. But despite her entreaty, the sun still made its way to meet the waters of the ocean, and her steps reluctantly slowed, feet wedded in perfect rhythm to the descent of the sun.

And then, as the sun sank below the glittering coral waves, she stopped.

11

The elephant was stationed by the gates of the temple waiting for him. As he stood by for the mahout to position the steps that would take him to the platform strapped to the elephant's back, Uthiyan heard a slight rustle. A short figure appeared behind him and quickly pressed a parcel into his hand. Before Uthiyan could react, the figure had vanished. All he caught a glimpse of was a palace servant's livery.

Baffled, Uthiyan unwrapped the parcel to find a fine green leaf, still glistening, covered with letters painted in vermilion.

> My wrists grow thin, the leaf read.
> And my bangles loosen
> I entreat you to save me
> From this fire that burns

That eats me alive
Tonight
This night
When the night watch changes
In the green grove covered with jasmine
Behind the statue of the goddess Kuttuvai

Could it be Madhavi? He could not think of another woman so bold in her desire. The girls of Vanchi, his mother's handmaidens, were experts in the art of coquetry, but none would dare be so audacious. No, those girls preferred to simper and giggle, obsessed with the games and stratagems of love, one moment appearing to be engrossed in their paramour, and feigning disinterest the next, springing a trap, with twists and turns, to snare their lovers.

It must be Madhavi.

The hours seemed to drag; and Uthiyan, restless, paced up and down the length of his chamber, reliving every moment of his last encounter with her.

He still could not understand the impulse that had made him stop. He had wanted her. Yet, when she was there before him, a dream come real, alive, breathing, he had stopped.

Why?

Was it the situation he was in, he wondered. There

had been that night, mingled with the desire, a sense of disquiet that had been impossible to ignore.

Had she wanted him because he was a prince?

There.

That was it.

He wanted her to desire him not because he was a prince.

He wanted to be more. More than a prince who had ascended to his position merely by the accident of birth.

He paused mid-step, startled.

Did that mean that he wished to be king? Prizes, war, valour, adulation, odes in praise of his bravery – is that what he wanted? To be the subject of great poems, like his ancestors, or a king who warred, like his father and his uncle Karikala Chola who had led his armies right up to the foot of the Himalayas?

Finally, the cry sounded that announced the change of the night watch. Uthiyan carefully opened a window, and after looping a knotted cord of rope around one ankle, he quietly slipped out on to the parapet.

He glanced up at the sky. He was in luck – the moon was just a faint blur of light, veiled by a tissue of cloud, and he doubted that any of the guards would notice him. Taking a deep breath, he grabbed hold of the closest swaying coconut tree that grew by his window, and flung his body on to the trunk. It had been years since he had done this, and he felt a twinge of regret – thinking of all the times that he and his brother had sought to flee the stifling attentions of the kadilapakkar, the royal guards. He wrapped his feet around the tree, looping and tightening the cord of rope around his ankle, and then, just as he used to when he was boy, shimmied down the length of the coconut tree.

A few minutes after he hit the ground, he made his way to the shrine of the goddess Kuttuvai.

He frowned as he approached the shrine.

Something was not quite right. He tensed. The shrine was usually lit, even at night, but the torches were out.

Perhaps Madhavi had arranged for that in an effort to ensure privacy?

He exhaled and relaxed. That had to be it. Cautiously, he threaded his way by the shrine and out behind to the grove.

The clouds completely obscured the moon. Blackness everywhere. All Uthiyan could make out were the heavy black shades of tree trunks and the merest white shimmer of jasmine. Carefully, he edged forward. There was a twitch between two trees, he thought. He squinted, and crept closer.

The sky shifted and the moon, now free, shone brightly. Uthiyan saw a figure, swathed in cloth, back towards him, a slender arm, bracelets glinting in the moonlight, resting against a tree.

'Madhavi?' he whispered.

The figure spun around at the sound of his voice. Uthiyan, shocked, jerked back – this was not Madhavi, this was not even a woman, this was a man clad in the robes and jewels of a woman.

Startled, he stepped back, into another hard body behind him.

He felt hands reach to grab his feet, and hold his arms fast.

And before he could even scream–

A gag was slipped over his face and tied roughly over his mouth.

What was happening?

Panic gripped Uthiyan and he pulled at the hands at his throat. When that failed he swung his heel back. There was a low grunt, as his foot connected with something soft, and the hold on him was released.

Uthiyan took his chance, and spun around to face his attackers – but another body barrelled into him from behind, and Uthiyan shrieked as, pushed to the ground, a knee ground into the small of his back.

'I watched your grandfather die on the battlefield, blood pouring from a million wounds, his back broken. He did not even make a sound once!' His assailant, scornful, pressed harder down.

Uthiyan screamed again. This time, goaded by the pain, Uthiyan squirmed and reached out to grab a fistful of cloth. Fabric ripped, and Uthiyan, still holding on desperately, rolled over, and sinking one hand into the earth around him, flung a fistful of mud into his assailant's face.

The man grunted again, blinded, and Uthiyan used his advantage to push him away, and rose to his feet.

But there were three others waiting for him, and they all bore down on him at once. One grabbed his legs, the other his arms, and the third punched him in the face.

Uthiyan was dragged through the grass and mud, and then found himself held, spreadeagled over a tree stump.

As he struggled, a glimmer caught his eye – the silver edge of a dagger, held close to his throat.

And then, as he watched, the hand that held the dagger drifted down to the parting in Uthiyan's dhoti, holding the blade over his groin.

'Shall we kill you or geld you?'

Uthiyan inhaled sharply.

Another man spoke up, the one holding his arms down. 'He's scared. I can feel him tremble.'

'Kill him.' This was another man. 'He'll talk if we just geld him.'

'We can cut his tongue too,' the first man protested, sounding like he was pleading.

'No, Neelakantan! Just kill him, and make it quick and clean. There is no reason to make him suffer.' Uthiyan almost felt a strange rush of gratitude for this man.

The dagger swept up again, towards his throat.

Uthiyan looked up at the face of the man who held the dagger, into a pair of feverish eyes and a sinister, crooked smile.

He screamed.

And everything turned black.

~

Uthiyan woke up, the metallic taste of blood in his mouth, bandaged and sore, in the palace infirmary. The commander of the night watch told Uthiyan that they had found him, unconscious, buried underneath the bloodied corpse of one of his assailants.

They took him to see the corpse, spread on the ground between two trees. A bloodied, mangled thing, mauled beyond recognition.

An eye had been gouged out, a piece of a ear torn off. A finger severed completely.

Uthiyan had shuddered and retched, while the commander had pulled aside the man's mangled uniform to reveal bloody lacerations. 'His name was Neelakantan.'

'Who did this?' Uthiyan asked.

The commander sighed. 'We were hoping you would know. Can you remember anything?'

Uthiyan shook his head. The last thing he remembered was the edge of the knife, glinting in the darkness. And only darkness after that.

'It must be the goddess Kuttuvai,' a younger solider, by the commander's side, piped up. 'She must have come to protect the prince.'

The commander shrugged. 'It must be that, whoever it was, praise be to them, for saving the life of our Komahan.'

There it was. That word. Komahan. Uthiyan shivered, and turned to the corpse again. 'Who was he?'

'A soldier,' the commander of the night watch replied, shamefaced. 'One of my own company.'

Uthiyan digested this. 'There were two others apart from him.'

'Ah. That will explain the other footprints. The commander shifted uneasily from foot to foot. 'The other two might be soldiers as well. I will dispatch men to check the barracks against the rosters, and find out if any men are missing.'

Uthiyan pursed his lips. 'So you think this may have been an assassination plotted by soldiers of my father's army?'

The commander fidgeted.

Uthiyan's voice rose. 'Why?'

The commander reverted to calling Uthiyan by his correct title. 'Ilango, there are men . . .' He stopped, cleared his throat, and began again. 'Forgive me for saying this, Ilango, I say this not as treason . . .'

'I understand.'

'But there are those who claim that you seek the ouster of your brother.' The commander paused. 'This is just a rumour, I merely repeat it. I have punished all those I have caught speaking such.'

Uthiyan nodded. Unbidden, a memory uncoiled – of a man screaming like a gutted pig, blood spurting from an open throat. A horrible sound. He shuddered.

'What is it, Ilango?'

'Nothing, just a passing faintness. Has my mother been here?'

'The Perumdevi visited when you were unconscious, and I have already dispatched messengers to her and the Ko with news that you are well.'

'I will go see her myself. Did my father come?'

'No, Ilango, he did not.'

12

Where was the queen? The handmaidens Uthiyan met in her apartments shrugged when he asked them, the servants busy polishing the carved wooden pillars of her pattimandapam did not know either. Uthiyan paced the corridors of the Silver Palace, bewildered, and worry began to knot and growl in the pit of his stomach. Could it be that, like him, his mother had been attacked?

Uthiyan raced to the small, little-used armoury in the Silver Palace, which doubled as a retiring room for palace guards. He placed his palm against the heavy wooden door, about to push it open when the soft rustle of a whisper, emanating from the room before him, made him pause. He knelt, his ear to the door, and caught the low, melodious murmur of his mother's voice. It was the last place that Uthiyan would have expected to find her. What was she doing in the armoury?

He pushed the door open and saw his mother, exquisitely and stylishly garbed in orange silk, her hair piled artfully into a bun on the left side of her head, fastened with golden chains studded with pearls.

The Perumdevi swivelled around, her garments whirling, as he entered – and catching sight of him, her face broke into a smile.

'Uthiyan!' She stepped forward and embraced him tightly. 'I am so glad that you are safe!'

Uthiyan returned her embrace, puzzled by the strange assembly of men in the small armoury. The sight of one of his mother's confidants, a goldsmith swathed in expensive silks, with fingers covered in gem-encrusted rings, perched on a stool far too small for his rotund posterior, was almost comical. But the other men present made Uthiyan wary – the Kadaikappalar chief in the queen's palace, a few of the leading men of Vanchi, a prominent fair-skinned Yavana merchant, one of the elusive Orrar, the spies in his father's service, and the chief commander of cavalry.

Why were such men of power meeting covertly in the dust-filled armoury with his *mother*?

'Mother, what's going on?'

Nalchonai's silks rippled as she turned. 'Excuse us for a moment.'

The men slowly rose, bowing to the queen, and exited the chamber.

Nalchonai turned to Uthiyan and clasped his hand to her heart. 'Son, ever since I heard of what happened to you last night, this heart of mine has been restless, gripped by pain, and I knew that I must protect my child. And I am not the only person to be so troubled by what happened to you. Scarcely had dawn broke before discreet messages came, and soon these men arrived, promising their help and support.'

His mother spoke innocently, winningly, but Uthiyan was disquieted by the sense, the premonition, lurking beneath her sweet love-filled words

He tore himself away from her. 'Why meet them here, Mother? In this room and not properly in your audience chamber?'

The pretence dissolved. 'Son, you know why. A kingdom with you at the helm. That is what I wish for, that is what I believe will keep you safe, and that is what these men want as well and they promise to keep you safe . . .'

'You are plotting against the throne?'

'No!'

'And who do you seek to keep me safe from?'

Nalchonai's eyes dipped.

'Who, Mother?'

'Your brother, Uthiyan. It is his soldiers who attacked you.'

'No, Mother! It is soldiers who resent the fact that I may be the next Ko.'

Nalchonai brushed his words aside with a flippant wave. 'It's the same thing, isn't it? What is the difference?'

'It's not!' Uthiyan crossed the room to grip her shoulders and shake her. 'It is not, Mother. If you can't see that – what are you doing?'

Nalchonai stared up at him, silent, wide-eyed, unable to understand.

Uthiyan gritted his teeth in frustration. 'What you are doing here is plotting, a conspiracy. This is wrong. This is absolutely wrong.'

'Son . . . they are loyal . . .'

'No.' Uthiyan walked away and opened the door of the armoury. The Orrar, standing with one ear to the door, almost fell down and Uthiyan found himself before his mother's co-conspirators.

Another situation to deal with. Uthiyan's heart almost sank. He was exhausted. So much had happened in a day. He had almost died, and here he was trying to put out the spark of a plot before it had time to flare up into something far more dangerous. He could barely stand, he felt so tired.

He struggled for the right words, and the correct, polite, diplomatic tone. 'Thank you for your concern, but my mother and I have no wish to inconvenience you in any way.'

With that, he strode out of the Silver Palace, not looking back, not wanting to see the expressions on the faces behind him. Why had they come to his mother? Not for him, no one truly cared about him, but they had come searching, scenting the promise of power, on a dare. A risk that could yield a reward.

That was it.

That was all it was. He was nothing more than a means to power, a way to advance, to fulfil unsatisfied ambitions.

Is this what it meant to be a king?

13

'Father, I renounce my claim to the throne.' Uthiyan rehearsed these words, over and over again, as he waited in the antechamber that adjoined the king's council chambers. Finally, the herald summoned him. The Ko was ready to receive the prince.

Now inside, facing the king, Uthiyan felt uncertain. 'Father,' he began, and then stopped. He shut his eyes, and breathed in deeply. 'Father,' he repeated, his eyes still shut, 'I have, after careful consideration, decided to renounce my claim to the throne.'

He opened his eyes now. His father was staring at him, intent, but there was no trace of surprise, nor any other emotion.

'Why?' the chief amaiccar asked.

'Last night I was attacked by soldiers who believe my brother is the rightful king. This morning, I received offers of support if I intend to press my claim,' Uthiyan replied. 'My fear is that as time passes, this will only increase in intensity and tear the kingdom apart. I have no wish to see that happen.'

'But the astrologer has forecast that you will be king,' the amaiccar responded. 'Is it possible to change fate? Is it possible for you to change the past or the future?'

'No,' the Ko finally interjected. 'A king cannot escape fate. He cannot run from death, nor can he run from justice. But Ilango seeks to run from his fate. He has played at being a prince, and for a while he sought to play at being a crown prince. Now, finding his life in danger, he does not find it to his liking, and wishes to exchange it for a pleasanter, safer path.'

Uthiyan gritted his teeth, and clenched his fists, but still the words could not be held back. 'Fate has caught you unawares too, Father. If you had chosen to be father first, you would find me better prepared to step into the role that you claim destiny has offered me. But you neglected to raise me the way you raised your other son. No, you left me to my own devices, and you have only yourself to blame if I fail to measure up to your expectations. You made me this way.'

The amaiccar gasped. 'No one speaks to the Ko like this!'

Anger bubbled up in Uthiyan. He had been within an inch of losing his life and his father did not care. He ignored the amaiccar and continued to face his father. 'You acted as the king, not as a father.'

'I have always been a king first, and then a father, Uthiyan, have you yet to realize that?' his father responded. 'That is what it means to be a king, that is what a king's dharma is.'

'Prince,' the amaiccar rose up now, 'as a member of the inner council, I must point out that what you say is dangerously close to treason.'

'What say you, *Father*?'

'I agree with the amaiccar.'

'Again you choose being a king over being a father. No matter. What I have said still holds. I renounce my claim and any right to the throne.'

'And how exactly will this be enforceable, Uthiyan?' his father asked. 'What of your descendants who may seek to press your claim in years from now, or that you may seek to on their behalf? Have you considered that? Or that your continued presence here may prove to be a deterrent to peace and unity?'

Uthiyan took a deep breath. 'So I promise not to produce any descendants. I renounce my claim to the throne, I renounce my title. I will leave this kingdom forever. I will take the vows of a celibate monk.'

His father did not blink. 'We accept.'

And that was that. Uthiyan turned to leave, but one last thought lingered, insidiously. He turned to face the king and his council once again. 'If I may be so bold as to ask one more question.'

'You may.'

'What would you have done, Father – let your sons battle it out and kill each other for this kingdom, for this throne?'

The Ko's face remained impassive. 'Yes. The strongest would have won.'

'Would it have been worth it?'

'It is the price that must be paid for the position.'

Disgust filled Uthiyan, swiftly followed by horror. 'I think it would have been convenient for you had I died last night.'

The king did not reply, but merely stared at his son.

Uthiyan walked out of the chamber.

His head was reeling. He paused, breathless, leaning his head against a carved wooden pillar. The palace swam before his eyes – the carved, gilded pillars, the shining teak floor, the garlands of jasmine and marigold, canopies embroidered with pearls and semi-precious gems, the brocaded garments of the courtiers, the gleaming swords of the palace guards.

This had been his entire life. This wealth, luxury, protection.

Had he just given it all up in an instant? What had just happened?

Uthiyan shook himself and pulled himself together, moving again. There would be time later to question, time to examine. But not now. First he must leave the palace.

'Ilango, wait!'

Just as Uthiyan, having exited the palace, neared the massive carved gates made of teak and iron, an attendant, panting, rushed to his side, bearing a swath of bark cloth and a razor. 'The king and the inner council send you this.' The attendant paused, suddenly shame-faced. 'They . . . they say that this is their command, that you take on the garments of a monk and shave your head before you leave.'

'Here?' Uthiyan replied, gesturing to the palace guards by the gate, watching this drama unfold, wide-eyed.

'Y-yes.'

Mortified, Uthiyan submitted to the attendant's attentions. First his hair was cut, and his head was shaved. And then his silken garments and golden ornaments were pulled off and replaced with the robes of an ascetic.

Uthiyan drew out his little dagger, carved with the Chera insignia of the bow and arrow, to put atop the pile of clothes and ornaments, but the attendant, now close to tears, pushed that back at the prince. 'No, Ilango, please keep that. It is not fitting that a prince walks into exile with no weapons to defend himself.'

News had travelled through the palace fast, Uthiyan realized, looking at the crowd of people gathered to watch his humiliation. He was close to tears, but he dared not let them show – not here, while he was in the palace grounds.

Attendants, courtiers and guards goggled and gaped at him as he passed through the massive gates.

At last he was out and walking down a tree-lined path, in orange robes, his head shaved.

'Uthiyan!' A shout made him turn round, and he saw Sattan, hurtling at breakneck speed through the gateway. 'Wait!'

Sattan, gasping, flopped on the ground by the side of the path. 'I heard a crazy story – one courtier passing it on to the next in the treasury, that you were walking out of the palace in the garb of an ascetic . . . that you had renounced the right to the throne . . . that the king had exiled you.'

Uthiyan nodded.

Sattan buried his head in his hands. 'I can't believe

this. We were drinking just a night ago, dreaming of the kingdom you would create. And now – this. I just can't believe it.'

'It's true.'

'Where are you going?'

'I don't know.' And it suddenly hit Uthiyan. All of it. The madness and confusion of the last few days. His fight with his brother. The attempted assassination. His mother's plot. His father's coldness. Now he was nothing, nobody, with no place to go to. His old life had been ripped out from beneath his feet.

He sank to the ground. And it was only when he felt the touch of Sattan's hand on his shoulder that Uthiyan realized he was weeping.

'We'll figure it out, Uthiyan,' Sattan said softly. 'We'll have wild adventures. We'll be mercenaries . . . where should we go? To Madurai to see the famous Neduncheliyan's famous Sangam? Or to Kaveripattinam? Or to the Himalayas, where we can finally determine whether Karikala Chola really did engrave the Chola tiger on to the side of a mountain?'

Uthiyan wiped his eyes, and smiled. 'But you're not coming with me.'

'Of course I am!' Sattan retorted. 'As if you even know where you're going as yet. You'd never figure it out without me. I think we should head to the harbour and offer ourselves as sailors on the Yavana ships, and set sail for the lands of the Yavanas. I hear the women there have hair the colour of gold and corals, skin the hue of pearls and milk, and eyes that can be mistaken for emeralds. Just imagine!'

Uthiyan, despite himself, could not help laughing. 'You're not coming with me,' he repeated.

Sattan rose and pulled Uthiyan to his feet. 'Of course I am. You can't stop me.'

'You can't.'

As they bickered, a palanquin passed them on the path, and then stopped a little ahead. A slender hand, dripping with gold ornaments, pulled back the curtain, to reveal Madhavi's lovely face.

'Prince!' she exclaimed, shocked, taking in the sight of his garb.

'I am no longer a prince,' Uthiyan replied. 'I've renounced my claim to the throne, and have just been exiled.'

'Who are you then, now?' The courtesan raised a quizzical eyebrow.

'I'm nobody, I think, for right now.'

'Where are you going, nobody?' Madhavi paused and glanced at Sattan. 'And nobody's handsome friend?'

Sattan preened.

'We don't know.'

'Well, then' – the courtesan turned to look at her small retinue, following the palanquin – 'why don't you come with us?'

Book 2

Ay

14

Darkness. Panting.

A white glimmer in the trees. The glinting edge of a knife.

Panic.

A man ahead, shaking in fear. A black shadow against more blackness.

The wide, wide whites of his eyes.

There's something else. Something beyond the trees.

Squealing. The sound of a pig being gutted.

The gurgle of blood.

Silence.

Stillness.

Uthiyan awoke, gasping for breath.

Beside him, Madhavi shifted, and then slowly turning, drowsily lifted her head up. 'The same dream?'

Uthiyan nodded.

Half-asleep, Madhavi pulled him to her and he turned to fit his face against the side of her neck. She felt warm, close – so alive after that dream of death. Her touch soothed him, and soon he found his hands drifting down, to the warm curve of her belly.

She inhaled sharply, now fully awake and her hips rose against his in a silent gesture of longing. He peeled back the layers between them, of smooth gold-bordered silk and rough-spun saffron cloth, and eased himself into her. They rocked together, her arms gently cradling him, in silence, in the small ship cabin.

Afterwards, Madhavi sunk back into a slumber, her arms still wrapped around him. Uthiyan though, could not sleep. He stared up at the ceiling of the small ship cabin. The walls seemed to close around him and he felt too hot to breathe. Carefully, he pried himself free of Madhavi, and picking up the small seven-stringed yal she had gifted him a few days ago, made his way out of the cabin and on to the main deck.

Stars sprinkled the night sky, and the small ship had been moored offshore, not far from the riverbank. Above, on the foredeck, Uthiyan could make out the sleeping forms of the other sailors, under leatherskin stretched tight between two poles, to protect them from rain and the sea.

Uthiyan peered over the side of the ship, watching

the moonlight glitter across the still Periyar river, broken by the occasional splash of a fish. He strummed the strings of his yal and began to hum the song that he had composed for Madhavi just that afternoon –

Witless swan! Keep away!
Do not come near!
Your gait cannot compare with hers.
Innocent swan! Do not approach!
Do not come so near to her!
You never can compete.
Stolid swan! Remain far from her!
Her game is men, and, for the hunt,
she haunts the confines of the earth
encircled by a tremulous sea. Oh, keep away!

She had loved it, and teased him by addressing him as 'my foolish swan' for the rest of the day.

It had all happened so easily. Like a dream, almost. A week ago he had been standing by the palace gates, lost and full of tears, and then she had passed by, and with a wave of her slender, braceleted wrist, his fate had been transformed – and he found himself aboard a fine, well-appointed, Yavana-designed galley, bound for the kingdom of Ay, where Madhavi would break journey en route to Madurai. And a few days later, his fate had shifted again, and he found himself in her bed. She had boldly teased him about their earlier encounter at the palace, and his reluctance, suggesting that other kinds of women were to his taste – or perhaps young men? In irritation and anger, he left her side. She had followed him, contrite, wishing to make amends. He had seized his chance, pushing her against the side of the ship and kissing her with all the roughness, anger and exasperation he felt.

She had kissed him back, responding with a tender sweetness that surprised him, and gentled his anger. He had stopped then, confused. 'I'm a nobody now,' he said, half in jest and half serious, astonished that she would still want him.

'I know,' she replied simply and pulled him into her chamber, and then into her bed.

But there had been a crease, something that still pulled at Uthiyan. For he could not miss the expression on Sattan's face as he watched Madhavi. No doubt about it. His friend, too, was besotted with the courtesan. Why wouldn't he be? She was intelligent and curious, beautiful and experienced, clever, talented and famous – so completely unlike the other girls and women they had known in Vanchi. Uthiyan knew that his friend fell in and out of love easily, one week he would claim to be sunk in the depths of gloom for the love of one of the queen's handmaidens, and then the next week Uthiyan would hear of his pursuit of a merchant's young, neglected wife in the city. But this still weighed on Uthiyan, for Sattan had given so much up for him.

The breeze brought a snatch of conversation and whispers, and Uthiyan looked up – at the mast – startled to see the object of his thoughts materialize before him. There, by the lookout, Sattan sat, keeping company with the Yavana sailor, who he had befriended early on in the journey – for Sattan was always beguiled and intrigued by stories of foreign lands.

Uthiyan made his way to them.

15

Their laughter quietened as he approached. Uthiyan could make out Sattan, beside him the Yavana sailor with the unpronounceable name, and Neelakantan, a sailor from Musiri.

'Uthiyan!' Sattan called out softly as he neared. 'Come, join us.' Uthiyan glanced at the hesitant faces of the two sailors, but it was a little too late to turn back now. Feeling like an intruder, Uthiyan sat down.

Sattan nudged the Yavana sailor, and he pushed forward a finely wrought Yavana urn, broken at one end. Merchandise broken en route, no doubt, before it could hit the port.

'It's not Yavana wine,' the Musiri sailor said, 'but something local.'

Uthiyan caught a whiff of something pungent,

with the sharp tang of spirits. He sipped it and then spluttered, coughing.

'Packs quite a punch, doesn't it?'

Uthiyan, eyes watering, could only nod.

'My friends tell me that if the current pace continues, we may land at Aykudi in the next two days,' Sattan said.

'Which is where we deposit our fair cargo, the dancer Madhavi,' Neelakantan added.

'Where do you go from there?' Uthiyan asked.

'We return to Musiri, just to reprovision and for a change of deckhands, before setting sail for my homeland west,' the Yavana replied.

'What cargo will you carry?'

'What the king of Ay trades with us – peacocks, tigers and other wild beasts from his mountain forests.'

'And you trade with him in goods.'

The Yavana shook his head. 'The king of Ay prefers gold. But I do not know what he does with it. I have been coming here for years and I have yet to see the people of Ay richer.'

'He plies poets and Brahmins with gold lotuses,' Sattan explained. 'He is renowned for his generosity. He gave our friend, the poet Paranar, an elephant once.'

The Musiri sailor snorted. 'What would a poet do with an elephant?'

'He sold it, although he had great trouble finding a buyer,' Sattan admitted. 'He said he hoped the next time Vel Pekan would stick to gold lotuses.'

'Do you not have such beasts in your lands?' Uthiyan was curious.

'Not as many as in yours. We have different kinds,' the sailor replied. 'Wolves and bears.'

'What do you do with the beasts you take from here?'

'Rich noblewomen vie to keep a peacock in their garden. But most of our cargo goes to the circus.'

'What is that?'

'A large fighting pit,' the Yavana struggled to explain, 'surrounded by seats for the public. In the pit, criminals and gladiators often fight the animals. The gladiators fight for money and for their freedom if they are slaves. The criminals fight for pardon. And the people watch for entertainment.'

Uthiyan was intrigued. 'You sound like you don't approve.'

The sailor touched the wooden cross dangling at his throat. 'I am a Nasiri, Prince. The Nasiri are not popular in the empire. Some have fled here, to Musiri, like me, to escape the persecution that we encounter.'

Riveted, Uthiyan turned to look at his friend. Sattan was listening intently to the sailor.

'We are treated like criminals for our faith,' the Yavana touched his cross again. 'The emperors hold that we must treat them like gods, and we do not hold with that. For the truth is that they are false gods, constantly sacrificing men and beasts to feed the unnatural, unsavoury appetites of their public. That is how the emperor holds on to power, courting the goodwill of the people through these bloody spectacles of gore and death. They feed us, the Nasiri, to the beasts when we deny that the emperor is a god.'

'You saw such a thing?'

The Yavana replied, 'Many years ago, when I was a young man. My ship had just come into port at Carthage, and then the city was gripped by the news that a young noblewoman – a beautiful and virtuous one – had claimed herself a Christian and refused to retract. She had just given birth to a child, and the child was taken, screaming from her breast, and this young woman was shut into prison with her two slaves, a man and a woman, who had converted with her, and who she had now claimed as her brother and sister.'

He paused. 'I was there in the crowd when they were taken to the circus. I witnessed what happened.

How the clothes were torn off the two women – and the slave woman had also delivered a child just two days ago. Her breasts were still dripping with milk, her body misshapen from childbirth.'

The Yavana shuddered. 'What sort of emperor would order this to happen? To such harmless, innocent, good women? And what crowd would want to watch these women humiliated and gored?

Neelakantan frowned. 'How do you believe in a god who did not save his devotees?'

'The miracle is their faith,' the gnarled, white-haired Yavana replied. 'Death is inevitable, but they met their deaths without fear. More than anything else I realized then God – my God – no good God can be on the side of emperors or kings who had innocent women gored to death in such a brutal fashion. I preferred the God of the Nasiri. He may not prevent my death, but he can give me the faith and the courage to make my way in this world.'

The Musiri man shivered. 'Enough of men and women being torn apart by beasts. I am glad I do not live in your country, my friend!' He took a swig of liquor and passed the jar to the Yavana sailor.

Sattan looked at Uthiyan. 'So what do we do on the morrow, friend, when we land at Ay? Do we stay or do we set sail for the western lands and its fighting pits? Or head to the northwest, to the Kalabhras lands that Paranar spoke of?'

'The Kalabhras?' Neelakantan spluttered and turned to Uthiyan. 'Prince, you best keep away from them! Stay in Vel Pekan's court. He will be generous and hospitable to a Chera prince.'

'No,' Uthiyan said. 'I've had enough of being a powerless princeling in a court. It is time to try something new.'

'To Madurai, then, to the Sangam?' Sattan smiled.

'A poet's dream, that is!' Neelakantan rejoined.

'Perhaps.' Uthiyan shrugged.

'The answer might be best decided, Prince,' the Yavana sailor now intervened, 'by this question: What is it that you want to be? A prince, a poet or a monk?'

Uthiyan stared up at the stars. 'Certainly not a monk. And I think I am done with being a prince'

'A poet then?' Sattan ventured.

Uthiyan thought of the tales he had heard of lands exotic and foreign. All the things he yearned to see. 'An adventurer first, I think.'

16

'No!' Madhavi was incensed, pacing the small cabin, in the midst of a swirl of billowing crimson silk, sweeping her jewellery and cosmetics into a carved wooden box.

Uthiyan sighed.

'It is a terrible idea to go up north. These *Kalabharas*,' she spat out the word, 'these northerners, do you know what they are like? They hate women. Song. Music. Dance. They are ascetics.'

'I am dressed like one,' Uthiyan quipped.

Madhavi shot him a furious stare. 'You don't know what you are talking about.'

And then, as changeable as the sea, she transformed, her anger melting away, and knelt before him. 'Come to Ay,' she pleaded softly. 'Come with me to Vel

Pekan's court. He will be so proud to have a Chera prince at his court.'

'And then what, Madhavi? It will start again, the plotting, the conspiracies. I do not want that.'

'Nor is it safe,' Sattan, quiet until now, added.

Madhavi frowned, considering this. A moment later, her brow cleared. 'Come to Ay, but not as a prince!' she exclaimed.

Uthiyan pointed to his garments. 'What? As a monk in the company of a courtesan?'

Sattan tittered.

'Not as a monk,' Madhavi pleaded. 'Come as a singer! As a musician to accompany me – after all, you sing so beautifully, Uthiyan!'

Sattan was not convinced. 'It still won't be safe. The sailors on this ship know who he is. Talk travels.'

'Well.' Madhavi smiled. 'I'm going with two men, aren't I? Sattan is my bodyguard and Uthiyan is my musician. And which one is the Chera prince?'

Uthiyan turned to Sattan who, brow furrowed, seemed to be considering this. 'Sattan! This is a terrible idea.'

But Sattan didn't respond. He turned to Madhavi instead, gesturing to the stubble on Uthiyan's head. 'How do you explain that?'

'That is easy. His mother was ill, and he took a vow that if she recovered, he would shave his hair at the shrine of Murugan,' Madhavi replied. 'Or something along those lines.'

'You can't be considering this seriously,' Uthiyan interjected.

But Madhavi seemed to have persuaded his friend. 'It will be more comfortable in Ay and certainly far more pleasurable than roaming up north.'

Sattan agreed. 'This makes sense. And I can take care of myself.'

Uthiyan was still dubious. 'Are you sure?'

'Yes.'

Uthiyan sighed. 'Fine, then.'

'And so it is!' Madhavi clapped her hands, delighted. 'Now gentlemen, out of here, for you are making a mess!'

The king of Aykudi sent an elephant and a company of guards to escort Madhavi, from the bank of the river up to his palace. But Sattan and Uthiyan had to make their own way, on foot, up the treacherous slopes of the hills of Ay.

Stopping exhausted at the top of a hill, gazing down below at the low huts of the fisherfolk that clung to the riverbank, Uthiyan spotted a terrace hung with drying nets.

He pointed. 'Now imagine a girl there, Sattan.'

And with that, he began to pluck the strings of his yal.

Beside the fisherfolk's low huts there lies
a terrace where the nets are left to dry;
and Death, concealed within a young girl's form,
her eyes as sharp as deadly arrowheads,
sits on the shore, there where the shining sand
is beaten by the lustful waves. She holds
a wreath of lovely flowers in her hand,
and sells her fish. Had I been told
she might be near, I would have not dared to come.

'Beautiful!' Sattan exclaimed, and applauded.

'Rubbish,' said another voice, a woman's voice, 'he scared the peacocks away!'

Uthiyan turned to see an old, grey-haired woman watching him. He laughed. 'Grandmother, where do you go?'

'To Ay, to visit the queen.' Amused by the quizzical expression on their faces, the old woman continued. 'She has sent for me.'

'Why?' This was Uthiyan.

'Her heart is breaking. So she turns to gods and the world of the spirits hoping that her heart and her husband will return. But her prayers have yielded no effect.'

Curious, Sattan asked, 'Is there a cure for a breaking heart, Grandmother? Do you know of one?'

Uthiyan glanced sharply at his friend. Was Sattan asking in jest? Or was he asking because of a broken heart?

The old woman sighed. 'The cure is simple. To disregard her husband. But to convince her to swallow this medicine will be difficult. But enough of me, young men, where do you go?'

'To Vel Pekan's court. We are in the company of the dancer Madhavi.'

'Ah! I suspect then that she is the same dancer that the queen fears will snare her husband's heart.'

'Does that make us enemies then?' Sattan quipped.

Uthiyan felt uneasy. 'Rumour has it that he has a fondness for dancers,' he added.

The old woman shrugged. 'Most men do.'

Sattan burst out laughing.

The old woman frowned, surprised. 'What's so funny?'

He gestured at her stocky figure and her ascetic robes. 'You, Grandmother, are a nun! What do you know of men and dancers?'

The old woman smiled ruefully. 'Now you see me grey-haired and stout. I was young once.'

Sattan rolled his eyes but Uthiyan was intrigued. 'What happened?'

'I had a husband, and Queen Kannaki and I have that much in common. I was exasperated enough to seek a spiritual life. Husbands have that effect.' She looked at them both suspiciously. 'Are either of you husbands?'

Both men shook their heads.

'Excellent,' the old woman exclaimed. 'Then we shall definitely get along well. Provided you stay that way. Husbands only cause grief.'

'You might be right there, Grandmother,' Sattan added, unable to keep the humour out of his voice.

But the old woman didn't take offence. 'Of course I am.'

17

The newfangled wealth of Aykudi – amassed through the tigers, peacocks and other animals for which Vel Pekan's hunters scoured the forests, and through the pepper vines that coiled around the trees that forested the slopes of Vel Pekan's mountain, to send on Yavana ships to distant shores – was on display in his newly built pattimandapam.

It was designed as a tribute to the same forests that were the source of the Vel's wealth – each pillar artfully carved in the shape of an animal, and patterned with the motif of a pepper vine. And so Uthiyan found himself gazing at a peacock, Vel Pekan's crest, beak emerging from the plinth, intricately painted blue feathers fanning across the width of the yellow pillar. On another, a lion growled, painted in gold, and on a third, a crocodile, rendered in shades of green and crimson, opened its jaws to reveal glinting silver teeth. Each was exquisite, but the effect of the whole was, as Sattan whispered, 'An assault on the eyes – as if Pekan had made money and wanted to spend it – in a hurry.'

As Uthiyan settled down, tuning his yal, the courtiers seemed to clash just as the colours of Pekan's hall jarred and warred. There were two camps: one gaudy and dressed flamboyantly, revolving around the corpulent figure of Vel Pekan, while the other – more sober and restrained – settled around Pekan's wife, sitting a marked distance away from her husband.

Madhavi entered, beautiful as always, clad in a vermilion silk, the brightness of which was lost amidst the garish frenzy of the pattimandapam. Pekan watched her from his seat on his golden throne with hungry eyes, his gaze travelling up and down the length of her body.

Kannaki – that was the name of Pekan's wife, Uthiyan recalled. She was pale, and sat with her back straight, prim, her mouth in an unmoving line, as if the dance was a penance that she had to endure.

The servants' hall had been a flood of gossip the previous evening – the dancing girl that Pekan had been infatuated with had lived in the next village. The poets, Kapilar and Paranar, had both taken Kannaki's side and had plagued Pekan with their poetry – begging him to disregard the dancer.

And he had.

Now there was a new dancer at his court. In anticipation of Madhavi's visit, one prominent noble's wife had visited Kannaki and begged her to undergo a pilgrimage south, to the shrine of Ayappa to beseech him to keep her husband in her bed.

But the pious Kannaki had shook her hand. 'No,' she had told her friend, 'my husband is my only lord!'

The gods would be offended by such talk, the serving woman who recounted this tale to Sattan and Uthiyan had believed.

Uthiyan's eyes now caught a flicker of movement at the end of the hall. There was the nun they had encountered earlier in the day, seated in the back, watching the performance with great relish.

A strange nun, that one, Uthiyan thought.

The performance ended, and Vel Pekan, after a thunderous applause, had beckoned Madhavi, and after a series of whispers, had exited the hall with her. Uthiyan's heart sank, but he schooled his features – and noticed that Kannaki was doing the same.

A few minutes later, a courtier approached him and Sattan. The Vel had requested his presence.

The courtier led them through a labyrinthine

network of corridors and apartments, and then stopped before one unassuming door. He paused and knocked, before ushering Uthiyan and Sattan in.

Uthiyan entered – and was astounded.

Every inch of space in this small room was covered in finely carved teak, panel after panel exquisitely engraved with images of copulation.

There were panels of mass, frenzied coupling – of rishis and apsaras, of men and rakshasis, of rakshasas and apsaras, of pisachas and bhootas, kings and queens, courtiers and eunuchs.

One man surrounded by a sortie of women in various positions and stages of undress.

Another spying upon a dancer as she coquettishly pulled up her lower garment.

Elephants rutting, snakes entwined around each other.

Gazelles mating, while a hunter aimed his bow at the male.

One of a man thrusting into a woman with the head of a tigress, and another where a woman embraced, impossibly, a swan.

Every single possible and impossible position and mix seemed to be catalogued on this wall.

Uthiyan exchanged a wide-eyed, incredulous glance with Sattan.

A low swing hung in the centre of the room, paired with a couch. Madhavi occupied the couch, sitting demurely, her feet daintily under her, while Vel Pekan reclined on the swing, his belly spilling over one side.

'So this is the young man,' Pekan drawled, his eyes drifting towards Sattan. 'This is the prince.'

Madhavi nodded, and Pekan subjected Sattan to close scrutiny, seeming to measure and weigh every detail of his appearance. Sattan straightened his spine, and attempted to look as regal, haughty and imperious as he could.

It was all Uthiyan could do to stop himself from laughing out loud.

Then Pekan thrust a fat finger in Uthiyan's direction. 'And this one can be trusted?'

Madhavi nodded again. 'He is my musician, he knows all my secrets.'

'Then play something for us, young man,' Pekan commanded.

Perplexed, Uthiyan began to strum a love song on his yal.

After a moment, Vel Pekan addressed Sattan in a soft tone, which Uthiyan strained to catch.

'Prince,' the Vel began, opening his arms wide. 'I welcome you to my court. Please be assured of every comfort here. I apologize to receive you in this fashion, but the spies of every king and chieftain in Tamilaham infiltrate my corridors like pests, and even my own wife is not above spying on me. I shall immediately have you placed in chambers more comfortable, although not what a prince might find suitable, but my friend' – and here he gestured to Madhavi – 'tells me that a disguise must be maintained.'

Sattan assented, playing along, and used flowery phrases to express his gratitude.

Pekan nodded, and using a bell placed at his side, summoned another courtier to escort Sattan to his new quarters.

Scarcely had Sattan left, when Pekan, now gesturing to Uthiyan to play louder, turned to Madhavi.

Uthiyan complied, but now could only catch snatches of the conversations.

It seemed that Pekan was enquiring into Sattan's motives for coming to his court.

Madhavi giggled. 'Out of love for me, of course, what else?'

Pekan shot her an assessing, shrewd look. 'That I believe, my dear, but there must be another reason as well. Perhaps he seeks to rally support against his brother.'

Madhavi shrugged.

'I wonder. I wonder.' Pekan pulled at his moustache.

'The Kalabhras, rumour has it, are marching here to take up arms against the Pandyan king. I have no quarrel with him. But a Chera princeling with a claim to the throne may make the Kalabhras turn their attention to the west.'

He paused, and poured a portion of Yavana wine into a goblet. 'A message arrived, just before you reached Ay, from one of my spies in Vanchi,' he continued, handing her the wine, 'that since your prince left, Shenguttuvan has quarrelled with his father. The queen is in disgrace. The Cheras are ripe for the picking.'

Uthiyan, startled by this news, skipped a note. Madhavi looked anxiously at him, but the king did not seem to notice.

Pekan continued. 'Do you think this prince might be willing to entertain an alliance with the Kalabhras?'

'I do not know.'

'We shall see.' The Vel patted her hand and then eyes slitted, favoured her with a more amorous glance. 'Is it true that the princeling is your lover?

'Yes, Pekan, he is.'

'Is he a jealous sort?'

'Very.'

'And is there no way I can pluck you from his arms?'

Madhavi flung back her head and burst out

laughing. 'I have the chance of becoming a queen, Vel Pekan, can you offer me that?' She took one last, long, leisurely sip from the goblet Pekan had handed her, and rose to her feet. Uthiyan followed suit.

The Vel shook his head ruefully, looking at her with longing. 'One wife is one too much.'

Lovemaking that night was fierce and desperate, Uthiyan seeking to erase all the touches, all the little glances that Vel Pekan had bestowed upon Madhavi.

Madhavi noticed.

'You must get used to this,' she chastised him afterwards. 'This is the nature of my trade.'

Her words felt like cold, hard stones sinking into his gut.

She had chased him out then, telling him that she could not risk him being found in her bed the next morning. Uthiyan had dressed in a hurry and made his way back to the servants' hall in the middle of the night.

But there were corridors and rooms filled with sprawling, sleeping figures, and Uthiyan, lost, found himself suddenly in a walled garden, where the moonlight fell on the figure of a young woman seated on a carved bench, her head buried in her arms.

She was sobbing.

He was about to approach her, but then she turned,

and he – following some mysterious impulse – had slunk back into the shadows.

But he could make out her tear-stained features in the moonlight.

A pale moon-shaped face. Eyes, red from weeping, shaped like a fish, under a pair of heavy, black eyebrows.

A mouth that hadn't smiled in years.

It was Pekan's queen. Kannaki.

Kannaki spoke, and Uthiyan could not see who she was addressing. 'I could live silently,' the queen said. 'I could live patiently. That's what they tell me, the old women, the young women, even the children. That I am so good. That I am' – and here her lips twisted in a sneer – 'a paragon of virtue. That the power of my chastity will draw my husband back to me, in time. Then, why, Kavunthy Adigal, why must I endure this?'

She pressed under her breast. 'This pain. It feels so sharp, like a dagger cutting into my flesh. It feels like a wound inside, but a wound that I cannot heal.'

She moved, and now Uthiyan could make out the figure she spoke to. It was the nun he had met earlier.

'Child,' the nun said. 'It is your karma. Something you did in a past life. And you must expiate this.'

'But this pain, this pain! Sometimes it is just dull, a discomfort. Sometimes it awakens me in the night, like a knife stabbing me. I wake up and turn, and I find that my husband is not there beside me. That I am alone. Moonlight falls on emptiness, on creased sheets and no man. And then the dagger twists.'

She covered her face with her hands. 'Sometimes I wake up sobbing. Oh, there are days when I hate him. I hate him, and I hate him. I wish I could run away. Return to my parents. Or that I could cast these things off, and take the vows of a nun and shave off my hair. But I know, even then, that I would care. That this pain that binds me to him will not leave me.'

Fat tears rolled down her cheeks as she wept. 'The worst is, I cannot help loving him. Loving him even though it hurts me, in spite of his numerous women, in spite of his terrible jokes. It is not a love of position, money or even desire. I cannot even explain it. Look at him – he was handsome once, but now he is fat and bloated. Nor is he gentle. Nor is he kind. Nor is he particularly good. And yet I love him. What is this? What is this that traps me? What is this that does not allow me to go free? What is this that I would sacrifice my happiness, my youth, even my life for? I do not understand it.'

The nun sighed. 'This is suffering.'

'Kavunthy Adigal, the worst of it is this rage. It is inside me. I know it is not seemly. It is not becoming of a woman to show her rage. So I keep it within.' Kannaki shook her head. 'It holds me and it does not let me go. It festers.'

She continued to weep. The nun laid a comforting hand on her shoulder. Uthiyan slid back into the shadows, determined to make his escape, but he must have not been as silent as he hoped for suddenly the nun's eyes flickered. She looked up and straight at him.

There was something in her gaze that held Uthiyan still for a moment, before he broke away and crept away to his quarters. Something ageless, timeless, all-knowing in her eyes.

18

What was happening? A palace attendant had woken Uthiyan, when dawn had scarcely broken, whispering that the Vel had summoned him. Uthiyan, stiff and aching from sleeping on a threadbare mat in a corner of the servants' hall, had roused himself, and then followed the attendant through a tangle of corridors, courtyards and rooms until he was in the outer room of the Vel's council chamber, waiting.

Why had the Vel called for him? The attendant wouldn't answer, and Uthiyan was soon distracted by the arrival of Madhavi, dressed in an expensive emerald silk, a golden mulaikaccu and a necklace of corals. Sattan followed in her wake, and then a guard signalled them to enter.

The king's council chamber was austere but Uthiyan's eyes swept past the Vel, past his bleary-eyed adviser, to rest upon a figure, bound and gagged, held between two soldiers. His eyes were bloody and bruised, and there was a nasty cut on his upper arm, and a gash across his ribs.

'That man,' the Vel announced, gesturing with one chubby hand, 'was apprehended outside your quarters.' His fingers travelled back to indicate Sattan, who was astonished. 'He was after the Chera prince.'

And then, the Vel turned to glare at Uthiyan. 'But little did he know that this man was not the real Chera princeling.' Pekan rose from his seat, and then, with one swift stroke, cut the man's throat.

Blood spilled out. A muffled scream escaped the man. His body crumpled to the ground. Uthiyan watched in horror as the blood pooled in crevices and then ran across the length of the chamber floor.

Red, red everywhere, lapping against the edge of the room, staining the fine teak floors of Pekan's palace, licking the edges of Madhavi's gold-bordered green silk. Sattan stared, ashen-faced, at a red splatter on the side of his arm.

The soldiers, without a flicker of surprise, bent to grasp the man's arms, and dragged the corpse out of the room, leaving a bloody trail behind.

Madhavi was the first to find her voice. 'Who sent him?'

The Vel shrugged. 'He told us, as assassins do, a pack of lies. But the chief of my palace guards caught him making his way towards your bodyguard's apartments – and so we surmise that he is not from the Chera court, as the chief of my Orrar informs me that he found not this man' – but now Pekan fixed his gaze on Uthiyan – 'but this one, slipping out of your bedroom.'

He paused and then pivoted to face Madhavi. 'Why would you take for your lover a simple musician, Madhavi, and then pretend that another man is your lover? No, that makes no sense.'

Then Pekan addressed Uthiyan. 'Prince, your enemies – whoever they may be – seek to find you even here. You cannot escape what has begun. Nor can you hide. Your life is not safe. And even if you choose to spend the rest of your life in exile, it will never be safe. I suggest that you consider, again, my offer – and that you meet with the Kalabhras ambassadors. I expect them to arrive shortly.'

Uthiyan felt trapped by his host. 'I will consider it.'

As they left the conference room, Uthiyan yanked at Sattan's upper cloth.

'So what should I do?'

'Not here,' Sattan whispered. He pulled him down the length of the corridor, and through another doorway, and then another and another. Finally, they were in the room that Sattan had occupied, a guest chamber designated for a prince.

'I wish Pekan had not killed the assassin before we could question him. He probably did that on purpose. To force your hand. But he's still right, Uthiyan. This will follow you,' Sattan said.

'Who do you think sent the assassin?'

'Someone in the court. Your brother.' Sattan paused, and then added, softly. 'Perhaps even your father.'

'*No*!'

'It's possible.'

Uthiyan struggled with the mixture of emotions this raised in him. 'Why do you say that?'

'The prophecy, Uthiyan. You can't disregard it. You cannot escape it. The entire court witnessed it. Neither your father's reign nor your brother's claim to the throne will ever be safe as long as you are alive.'

'What should I do?' Uthiyan stared at Sattan, desperate.

'I don't know. I think you will have to play politics,' Sattan replied.

What were his options? Seek shelter with his uncle at Kaveripattinam? Strike a deal with the Kalabhras?

'The Kalabhras.' Uthiyan paced the length of the room. 'Pekan will meet with them.'

'Perhaps you should too.'

Uthiyan mulled over this. He came to a halt. 'It may buy us some time.'

Sattan chuckled. 'You wanted to go there, didn't you? But Madhavi persuaded you to come here. Perhaps your fate is coming to meet you here.'

Uthiyan heaved a deep sigh. He had no idea what fate or this prophecy meant for him. 'Perhaps.'

19

Clouds, gathering low on the horizon, clustered around the blue mountain peaks. The scent of an approaching storm, wild and feral, infused the breeze that swept through the garden. The queen, sitting on an intricately carved wooden bench, surrounded by her handmaidens, demanded that Uthiyan – like the other poets who visited her husband's court, entertain her with poetry. Uthiyan was uncertain. All he could sing was love songs, and that, he suspected, would not be to this queen's liking. He strummed his yal, and began singing a song of separation, suited to the windswept trees and creepers of her mountainside garden.

The queen listened, sorting through the basket of red kurinji flowers on her lap, twining thread around their stalks as she fastened them together into a garland.

Uthiyan's gaze drifted, spying a couple strolling on a garden path towards them. His breath knotted in his chest, the way the woman moved, leisurely and graceful, was unmistakable. It was Madhavi. And she laughed, as her partner whispered something to her.

Who was it? The man faced away from him, and Uthiyan, impatient, craned his neck to get a better look.

Was it Vel Pekan?

No. It was his friend, Sattan. Madhavi laughed again.

Uthiyan, seized by jealousy, stumbled on the words of his song, his fingers striking the wrong note.

Kannaki noticed this. 'You love the dancer, don't you?'

Uthiyan stared blankly at the queen.

'It's obvious. It's in the way you look at her.'

Uthiyan, uncertain, picked up his yal again, but the queen gestured for him to lay it aside.

She too watched Madhavi, and then with another wave of her arm, dispatched a handmaiden to call the dancer to her.

When Madhavi approached, the queen smiled

sweetly. 'We just watched you laugh – and both I, and your friend here – wished to know what made you laugh so.'

Madhavi turned to Sattan. 'He sang me a poem.'

Her smile felt like a knife twisting in Uthiyan's chest.

'Will you sing it to us?' The queen addressed Sattan, who looked a tad foolish.

He demurred, but Madhavi, laughing, reached for Uthiyan's yal. She began to sing.

> Like the evening, you make me go mad.
> Sneaking in when the ruler of the day has left,
> And bringing sadness to a world that has only
> asked to
> Close its eyes and forget.
> You trouble my thoughts and drive me mad.

The queen politely praised Sattan's song. Uthiyan too mouthed praise, but within he was furious. Jealous because of the way Madhavi looked at Sattan. Angry too that Sattan's composition – to be honest – was a good one.

Kannaki seemed to sense this, for she invited Uthiyan to amble through the garden, back to the palace, with her. A handmaiden followed behind, discreetly, clutching the half-finished garland the queen had been making, leaving enough spacc for the queen to speak privately with Uthiyan.

'You know of my grief. Others have written about my grief, but their poems have failed to move my husband's heart. What use is a poem then? He praises the words, and gifts the poets elephants and golden lotuses. How true are these songs of grief and love then?'

'They are meant to entertain, to gladden – to pass the time . . .'

'No.' Kannaki shook her head. 'You speak of poems that are meant to wrangle rich presents from kings and their ilk. But that is not what makes a poem great. Nor is that what poetry is for.'

The queen had piqued Uthiyan's interest. The few poems he had written so far were of love and beauty, or describing moments – a storm, a quivering leaf. He had never considered the object of what a poem might be – that it could be something greater, that there could be a focused intent behind a poem. For him, the object was to write a poem that would win the admiration and respect of others. To win fame, a place at the Sangam in Madurai. He knew that Paranar saw something more in his poetry – an attempt to bridge the distance between the common man and the king.

Avvaiyar, from the stories he had heard, like Kapilar and Paranar, had at times scolded her patron, and at other times fought for him with her words.

He turned to the woman beside him. 'What is it for?'

Kannaki was silent for a few minutes, and then answered. 'To remember. To remember not merely what happened – but to *feel* what happened. To make us feel the sadness, the grief, the joy. To move us.' She asked, 'Why do poets tell stories to kings?'

Uthiyan pondered over this. What was the answer that Kannaki expected? He did not know, although he knew that she had beseeched poets to use their craft to win her husband back.

Was that what she meant?

But in his father's court it was different. Poets sang of his exploits, and the wars that his ancestors had fought – those were the poems that Uthiyan's father, if he deigned to listen to poetry, preferred.

Different kings liked different poems. But what did Kannaki think? 'I have not thought of this before, Queen. Why do you think we should tell stories to kings?'

'To make them feel. To move them to sympathy, to move them to action, to encourage them to good and virtuous deeds. To energize them with courage and valour. To inspire them to love. That's what poetry and stories are for.' Kannaki spoke with passion.

'Perhaps you are right.'

Kannaki stopped and looked directly at Uthiyan. 'Then write a poem, O poet, that describes my grief, to make my husband realize my plight. Write a poem that will make him a better husband, a better man, a better king.'

Uthiyan nodded, although inwardly, his heart sank. This had been done before, by poets greater than him, but it hadn't effected a lasting solution. What could he do? All he could do was try again.

They walked a portion of the way in silence before Kannaki spoke again. 'Kapilar – do you know of him?'

'Of course, he is one of the most famous poets alive.'

Kannaki smiled, a small bitter smile. 'He was a good friend to me. He tried to intervene with the king – but it didn't work. News came a few days ago. He died.'

Uthiyan, stunned, stopped. 'How?'

'You know that his patron, Vel Pari, was besieged for years at Parambu. Vel Pari was killed in combat, leaving behind two daughters. Kapilar took care of them until he found them a husband – and then he killed himself.'

Uthiyan frowned, upset. 'Why did he kill himself?'

'Because he blamed himself,' Kannaki replied, her voice breaking. 'Because Vel Pari had sent him to plead with the besiegers to break their siege, but he was unsuccessful. If he had succeeded, perhaps Vel Pari would still be alive.'

She was silent for a few moments, before continuing. 'But his death makes me so angry! Why did he have to kill himself? When he died, I lost the only true friend I had.'

~

That night Madhavi performed, and Uthiyan, as usual, accompanied her. But Madhavi's performance was off, and Uthiyan missed a note here and there. Though Vel Pekan smiled, and appeared to be delighted, Uthiyan couldn't help but feel that the real cause of Pekan's delight was that he had got Uthiyan where he wanted him – in a tight spot.

'He does,' Madhavi replied, when Uthiyan confided this suspicion to her as they made their way back to her room. 'But he is offering you a good deal.'

Uthiyan wasn't so sure. He didn't trust Pekan, but he was curious to know what Madhavi thought. 'You think I should do this? Go against my father? Go against my family?'

'Yes. Perhaps this is what the prophecy meant.'

'You believe it?'

They reached the entrance to Madhavi's room, and Madhavi paused before stepping over the threshold. 'Yes, I do.'

Uthiyan shook his head in denial. *He* didn't believe it. 'You can't possibly believe–'

Madhavi turned to look at Uthiyan, meeting his eyes. 'Uthiyan, can you escape your birth? Your fate? It will circle back to reach you here. It has already. Luckily, this time you are alive. But perhaps, not long from now, there will be another assassin.'

Uthiyan's eyes blazed. 'War, that's what Pekan is talking about. Bloodshed, dead soldiers and widowed women. My own land, my own kingdom, my own home – torn apart.' His voice rose. 'How can I want that? How is it right to even want that?'

'You are a prince, born from a line of warriors who gave their lives to defend your kingdom. War would come, anyway, in one form or another.'

'I don't want that!'

'Then what do you want? Uthiyan, you were not raised to live the life of an ordinary person. So how will you live? Running from court to court, king to king, and living off them?' Madhavi's words stung.

When Uthiyan did not reply, she continued, relentless, without sympathy. 'If you will not be a prince – then do you wish to be a musician? Or do you want to start playing poet? Or would you like to go back to being a monk? Perhaps that role fits you best.'

Uthiyan felt rage stir inside him, but he held it back, speaking through gritted teeth. 'Why are you pushing this? Why do you say these things?'

'Because you are *playing*, still, at life, Uthiyan. You cannot escape making a decision.'

Her words hit their mark. He slammed his fist into the wall beside the doorway. 'You are cruel.'

'No, I care about you.' She reached up to touch his face, but he brushed her hand aside.

'This is what you want, Madhavi,' Uthiyan spat back in anger.

She shook her head. 'No, that is certainly not what I want.'

'No,' Uthiyan kept on, determined to hurt her as she had just hurt him. 'That is exactly what you want – isn't it? That's why you've had me in your bed. Because I am a prince.' And Uthiyan found that he was voicing, finally, a fear that had been brewing in him, growing in him, all this while. 'And I could be king, and that would make you a queen.'

Madhavi stared at him, her face impassive.

This only pushed Uthiyan further. The memory of her laughing with Sattan came upon him and goaded him further. 'If it wasn't me – you would go with my friend, wouldn't you?'

Madhavi slammed the door in his face.

20

Madhavi!

She was so exasperating. It was difficult to breathe, even now, thinking of her. Uthiyan felt like a cord had been wrapped tight somewhere in his chest, stopping his breath short. He paced up and down in Vel Pekan's terraced palace ground, the moon overhead wrapped in a fine gauze of clouds.

Madhavi!

She was beautiful, fiery and passionate. Her fire was too much for him. Perhaps he would be better free of her. This was not the first time he had thought of this. She disturbed him. Obsessed him. Compelled him to act.

This passion left him no peace.

'Madhavi!' he growled.

'What was that?'

Uthiyan stopped short at the sound. It seemed to come from the garden. Someone else was up there. He stepped into the shadows and peered up. Who was there? It was a woman's voice, strained and slightly tense. Uthiyan silently crept into the garden to see a swing set up on the level above him, on which two figures, a man and a woman, sat.

'It must have been an animal,' the queen murmured. She turned back to her husband. 'And what is this with that prince who pretends he is a minstrel?'

Uthiyan, a chill running down his spine, realized that she was talking about him. Curious to hear more, he scuttled closer, until he was right underneath the royal couple, and impossible for them to see him.

The king didn't answer, so the queen continued. 'He is in love with her, don't you know?'

A slight creaking. Uthiyan imagined that above, on the swing, Pekan shifted uneasily. 'With who?'

'The courtesan.'

'Perhaps.' The swing creaked again, and it seemed as if the king was uncomfortable in his seat beside Kannaki. 'Maybe we can use him then. With the Kalabhras.'

'Is that right? What you are meddling with can come back to bite you.'

Pekan replied curtly. 'It is not your place to question me. That is not the order of wives.'

'But it is my place to care!' Kannaki objected. 'It is my place to advise you, because I love you.'

Pekan did not reply. The silence grew, and the queen spoke again, her tone contrite. 'Husband . . .'

'What is this, Kannaki?' To Uthiyan the king sounded more than merely irritated; he sounded weary. 'Do you care for the feelings of the prince or are you jealous of another woman?'

Another short pause. 'I speak out of love for you.' Uthiyan heard the words, but they sounded strained. As if Kannaki was gritting her teeth. Could it be that she was jealous? Or that she was worried about him?

Or both?

'Love.' It was the king who spoke, a trace of bitterness in his tone. 'Your love is like a noose around my neck and yours.' His voice rose, angry. 'Your love is so bold as to advise me what to do, when the fate of the world hangs in the balance!'

'My husband, I only seek to counsel you. For I am not merely a queen, I am also the daughter of kings. And I know this much – dharma comes to all. Dharma visits kings, most often, in the shape of death. And I fear that for you.'

'Kannaki! You have me do the "right" thing – but what is it that is in my interest and that of my kingdom? These two things are not always the same. The "right" course of action does not always bring profit and peace to me, my kingdom or my people!'

The queen wisely remained silent.

'Is this love, truly, Kannaki?' The king spoke, but his voice was desolate. 'Your virtue is supposed to add to my glory and honour, and here it is dragging me down. What would you have me do, Kannaki, for the love of you? I have given up other women. Now you wish me to give up my mind, and devote myself entirely to you and follow your counsel in my kingship? That is not love.'

A creaking again, and Uthiyan imagined that now the king had risen.

'Wait!' the queen cried, but there was no response, only a door banging shut a few moments later.

Kannaki burst into tears.

Uthiyan couldn't bear the sound of her weeping. He crept out of the shadows to head back towards his quarters. But as he made his way out of the garden, the moon, finally free of clouds, shone white and silent, and Uthiyan was startled by Kannaki's face, before him, gleaming white in the darkness. Unsettled, he tripped over a tree root, only to gaze up at the half-finished figure of an apsara carved into the side of a tree. Her face, glinting in the moonlight, looked to Uthiyan that the sculptor had used Pekan's queen as a model.

Her eyes were sightless, and her arms were extended in desperate entreaty, but bound by a creeper that climbed up the length of the tree to wrap around Kannaki's braceleted wrists and down her half-finished legs, as if rooting her in this place.

21

A pretty slip of a girl, one of the maids assigned to Madhavi, was waiting for him at his quarters, yawning and slightly cross at having had to wait for him for so long. She handed him an ornate garland of flowers – red, white and pink, knotted skilfully together, interspersed with bright green leaves. It did not take long to guess who this garland was from – for the delicate five-petalled pink flower was a signature of sorts – it was called madhavi-lata.

The verses, inscribed in red paint on the broad leaves woven through the garland, were as artful as the garland itself.

This night is unendurable
Torture for those who are left by their lovers
Can't you understand my pain?

'My mistress asks for a reply,' the pretty girl lisped. 'She hopes you will respond.'

So pretty, so coquettish, so demonstrative, so showy, thought Uthiyan, anger waking within him – and so unreal. So artful, just like Madhavi herself. There was performance, that dramatic nature – but what was behind that?

Nothing.

This was the art, the words, the behaviour of a courtesan.

Uthiyan reread the verse, a faint sickening sense of disgust rising within him.

A few months ago, perhaps even just a few moments ago Uthiyan would have been seduced by such an extravagant gesture.

But now something else stirred in his mind, the memory of Kannaki's tears. Of her pain.

That was real.

This wasn't.

The girl left, and still Uthiyan brooded. Madhavi was a superb dancer, a talented actress, a wonderful poetess.

He had seen her fake swoons. He had seen her pretend to be a rampaging elephant, a simpering princess, an abandoned wife, a wise king, a raging goddess, a budding lotus – he had seen her perform a hundred parts, and all of them believably. She was masterful at her art.

So how could he trust her? Was this just another performance? How did he know, how could he believe that what she said was the truth, not a part she wished to play?

She had accused *him* of playing at life – but it was she, he thought now, who was the one playing!

Suddenly, with a shock, another message – so oddly similar – came to his mind. It felt so long ago, but Uthiyan realized that it had only been a few weeks. From that night, after Madhavi's performance, letters painted in vermilion, letters that had driven him to the goddess Kuttuvai's shrine.

And straight into a plot to assassinate him.

Could Madhavi have actually written that letter?

But she couldn't have. She was his lover, his confidante now.

He dismissed the thought, but it continued to plague him.

Could she be plotting something larger?

Did she seek to make him her pawn? And whose pawn was she?

~

Sometime close to dawn fell asleep but his sleep was fitful, his mind turning memories over and over and over.

A white glimmer in the trees. The glinting edge of a knife.

Panic.

A man ahead, shaking in fear. A black shadow against more blackness.

The wide, wide whites of his eyes.

There's something else. Something beyond the trees.

Squealing. The sound of a pig being gutted.

The gurgle of blood.

Silence.

And then Uthiyan was running, running as fast as he could, his pulse racing, roaring in his ears, through the forest.

Suddenly he stopped in front of a statue veiled by darkness.

A statue of a woman, that much he could make out.

He must be near the shrine of the goddess Kuttuvai.

The moon burst free of the clouds and shone between the trees, moonlight creeping up the length of the statue to illuminate the face of the goddess.

But it was not the face that Uthiyan expected to see – the wrathful face of the goddess.

No, this was another face, familiar and human, eyes sightless, and something in her expression begging for help.

This was Kannaki's face.

22

A palace guard roused Uthiyan hours before daybreak, and in hushed tones informed him that Vel Pekan had sent for him. Uthiyan looked out – it was still night, darkness shrouded the peaks and valleys of Pekan's mountainous kingdom. Mystified, Uthiyan readied himself quickly and within a short period of time, found himself outside, by the elephant stables, clambering atop an elephant that Vel Pekan was already seated on.

'Where do we go to?' he asked Pekan.

'To meet the Kalabhras envoys,' the king replied tersely. 'They have a small force encamped in a valley some distance from here.'

'Why do they not come here?'

Pekan sighed. 'To avoid the eyes and ears that lurk at my court and are in the pay of other kings.'

Uthiyan brooded on this. Pekan clearly meant to put him in play, and had decided to throw in his lot with the Kalabhras.

Why?

As the pink tinge of dawn began to conquer the darkness, Pekan hailed the elephant to stop. There, in valley below them, was an encampment. Uthiyan had seen nothing like it before, no king's army in Tamilaham had ever resembled this – for the camp was orderly, built in the shape of a square around a cross, tight and compact, easy to pull down and build up again. The greatest surprise was the absence of musicians, clowns and dancing girls – a horde that numbered in the hundreds, following in the wake of the army, great luggage wagons behind them, like the way Uthiyan's father went to war.

'This is different,' Uthiyan finally managed to say to Pekan.

Pekan was unmoved. 'It is like the way the Yavanas make war. Not like we do. It means the Kalabhras can move faster and more stealthily across the countryside.'

'Everything will change,' Uthiyan whispered, staring down at the camp. The armies of his father and his uncle set to war accompanied by legions for entertainment. This was a lithe army, and as Pekan said, it could move fast. It wasn't weighed down by baggage trains and camp followers. How would the Cholas, the Cheras and the Pandyas – used to making war so differently – combat this?

'Perhaps, I do not know,' Pekan replied, guessing the train of his thoughts. 'We must respond to the new ways, we cannot keep with the traditions of the past merely because they come from the past. If we do so, we destroy ourselves.' He clapped his hand on Uthiyan's back. 'We have to adapt if we mean to own the future. You too, Prince.'

~

They descended into the valley. Uthiyan looked curiously at the Kalabhras soldiers – they were no different from any other kind of soldiers he had seen in his father's train, or in the company of his uncle. The Kalabhras emissary who met them led them to the heart of the camp, where a soldier, dressed in the shining bronze armour of the Yavanas, whirled about, a practice sword in hand as he battled three other soldiers in ordinary leather cuirasses.

Uthiyan watched, wonderstruck. The soldier, in his bronze armour moved with fluid grace, like a dancer. Uthiyan thought of Madhavi, then at the temple of

Agastya near Musiri, how she had changed into a pillar of molten gold. This man, though, was a bolt of lightning, swift and lethal, darting between his assailants, leaping in the air to parry one blow and then deal another. War was another kind of dance, Uthiyan thought, just more lethal.

He had never seen anything like it before. The soldier, gleaming in his armour, spinning like a second sun, flowing like a sun-dappled stretch of water, was something beautiful to behold. Uthiyan was mesmerized.

Beside him, Pekan shifted. 'What is the point of this?'

The Kalabhras envoy smiled, and clapped his hands. The fight stopped. The soldiers paused, mopping brows, exhausted.

~

'Prince!' Uthiyan saw Pekan hailing him, the Kalabhras envoy beside him. 'We must return soon, before our absence is commented on.'

Uthiyan, reluctant, made his way over to them. The envoy spoke again. 'Prince, I believe you are on the run. Aren't you?'

Uthiyan replied hesitantly, 'I am.'

'You see what our forces can do.' The envoy smirked, and turned to Pekan.

'Ally with us,' Pekan spoke. 'We will restore you to your kingdom.'

Uthiyan felt the pressure tightening in his chest. 'I do not wish to spill the blood of my family. Or anyone else.'

'But blood must be spilt, if not theirs, eventually it will be yours,' the envoy replied. 'Think on it, Ilango.'

'I will.'

~

That night, Pekan summoned Uthiyan to the chamber where he had first encountered the king, adorned with the carvings of humans, animals and half-human beings in coitus.

'They will change Tamilaham, Prince,' Pekan whispered to him. 'The world we know will disappear. Something else will come in its place, I know it, I can smell it. You should consider which side you want to be on. It is obvious who will stand to be the victor.'

You must deal with this cautiously, a voice sounded in Uthiyan's head. The Kalabhras were powerful, Uthiyan acknowledged, but it was another thing to bring this power to bear on his family, on his kin, and to see the men he knew perish under their swords simply so that he could be king.

A contrarian voice responded in Uthiyan's head – with or without him, war was coming. Could he remain apart from these events?

He needed to think more on this.

As Uthiyan made his way through the palace's labyrinthine corridors to his quarters, he ran into the nun exiting Kannaki's chamber.

'How is the queen?' he asked her.

'Half-mad with rage, half-grieving.' Kavunthy sighed.

Uthiyan, surprised, raised an eyebrow.

'Prince, may I venture to offer you a word of advice?'

Uthiyan flinched back. 'I am no prince–'

Kavunthy continued, ignoring his protestations. 'She is an ignored wife, she seeks power and the attention of her husband. And so she schemes and makes plans that go around and run contrary to his, and it worsens things between them. Right now, you are a knot between them. Some part of her believes that she would make a more righteous ruler than her husband.'

'Would she?' Uthiyan couldn't help but think having

seen Pekan's lustful nature, and his machinations first hand, that, in fact, Kannaki would make the right, just ruler.

Kavunthy lifted her arms and shrugged. 'Who knows? Perhaps a better ruler to the common folk, certainly. But she is not one who knows the best way to dabble in the intrigues of court, in the business of war, or making trade. That too is the task of a ruler.'

Uthiyan exhaled. 'By that standard, Adigal, I would make a terrible king.'

Kavunthy looked up at him. 'That you would, indeed.'

Uthiyan was piqued by her agreement, having half expected her, like all other courtiers, to demur. Was this the way to speak to a prince? 'Who are you? And how do you know who I am?'

'It is obvious. It is like trying to pretend a ruby is in fact a piece of red stone from a river. And who am I? I am what you see – merely a nun.'

Uthiyan was not convinced. 'You know far too much of the world, of queens and kings and courts, for me to be satisfied with that response.'

'What does it matter who I am?' Kavunthy smiled. 'But if you insist, I was a courtesan once, like your Madhavi.'

Uthiyan was dumbfounded.

'Yes, one desired by kings and princes, like she is now.'

'And then what happened?'

'I grew weary of it.' She said nonchalantly.

Uthiyan burst out laughing. Kavunthy shot him a roguish smile.

'But enough about me, Prince, you are the real source of mystery here.'

'What do you mean?'

'What will you do here?'

Uthiyan shook his head ruefully. 'I do not know.'

'But you must, Prince,' Kavunthy persisted. 'For we have a drama all set to happen – an estranged, righteous queen who wants you to plead her cause, particularly since now you are a prince, with a claim to press, and for that reason her husband may heed your words. Then there is the king, an unfaithful husband, who seeks to use you as a tool to advance the value of his kingdom. Your lover Madhavi – I do not know where her interests truly lie – perhaps with herself. And then your friend, who is steadfastly loyal to you, but is foolish and besotted with your lover. Your uncle, in pursuit of you to bolster his own power games with the Cheras. And then the Cheras themselves, divided between you and your brother.'

Uthiyan smiled grimly. 'You seem to know all my troubles.'

Kavunthy chuckled. 'Ah Prince. We forgot the Kalabhras.'

Uthiyan was taken aback. His surprise must have shown, for the nun chuckled again.

'What do you know of them?' Uthiyan asked.

'The queen believes that the king seeks an alliance with them, and will use you to cement that alliance. But the king would be wise to be wary of them.'

'Why?'

'They want all of Tamilaham. Not just a part of it. The lands of the three crowned kings and everything else in between too, including Pekan's patch.'

Uthiyan let out a low whistle. 'They want the whole world, then!'

'They seek an empire. They seek to change the world as we know it.'

'Into what?'

Kavunthy shrugged. 'That I do not know.'

Uthiyan thought of what Pekan had said of the Kalabhras, how they were a force of change that could not be resisted or stilled. 'Perhaps their world will be better than ours.'

'No, Prince, forgive me, I do not believe that. For them beauty is a sin, not a gift,' Kavunthy replied.

23

Shouts awakened Uthiyan.

He rose to a scene of chaos and frenzy. A mass of people – courtiers, servants, soldiers – were rushing through the palace, into the garden, to the riverbank. He let himself be carried by the stream of people. What was happening?

'It's the queen,' a servant girl told him. She was crying. 'It's the queen,' she repeated.

The crowd stopped by the banks of the river. There in the distance, he could make out something floating – it was a body, borne aloft by the river's current.

A soldier dashed into the water, wading against the current. A cook, standing next to Uthiyan, took off into the water as well, and soon Uthiyan too found himself in the river, struggling against the icy-cold current, to reach the body.

Uthiyan was now close enough to see that it was indeed the queen – Kannaki herself. But she was covered in gold, heaps and heaps of it – earrings, innumerable rings, a heavy belt, golden necklace after necklace, weighed down with emeralds and diamonds and rubies – as if she had chosen to wear the whole wealth of Pekan's kingdom.

Uthiyan was astounded. But it was not just Uthiyan. 'I never saw her wear so much jewellery,' a young boy exclaimed to the cook beside him.

'It was to help her drown, son,' the cook, his shoulders drooping, replied wearily. 'So that the gold and jewels drag her down.'

They struggled to haul her out of the water, but the jewellery and the clothing had tangled with the river plants and stones. She was stuck. They could not get her out. Was she still alive?

It was as if the river would not let her go.

Uthiyan, feeling helpless, siezed the opportunity to act. He dove in and caught a glimpse of her foot trailing a river creeper. He pulled at it, but it was caught in the heavy anklet that adorned her foot.

'Quick!' someone shouted. He could hear it, even under the water. 'Get her out! She is still breathing.'

There was no time, so Uthiyan tugged desperately at the anklet, but it remained stuck.

What could he do? He clutched the anklet, and by some feat of superhuman, desperate strength, the gold bent under his grip and buckled. The anklet broke – and jewels scattered out, tumbling into the riverbed, a cloud of diamonds, rubies, emeralds and pearls dissolving into the river.

Uthiyan was stunned momentarily by the gems, catching the light underwater, dazzling him before they set adrift, swallowed by the river.

He rose from the water as Kannaki was being pulled on to the muddy riverbank, her wet clothes and hair dragging behind.

She was unconscious. As her body was laid on the riverbank, her clothing fell askew – and the crowd gasped.

Uthiyan stood on tiptoe to see. The clothing had fallen to reveal Kannaki's right breast – a red, festering, painful, oozing mass.

Shrieks punctured the silence. A woman in front of him screamed and fainted.

24

'She's dead.' Uthiyan said to Madhavi, anger surging within him.

'Two nights ago, Madhavi, I received a letter. Did you write it?'

Madhavi jerked back, surprised by the sudden shift in subject. 'Yes, I did.'

'And the letter that other night, in Vanchi – the letter that sent me into a trap. Did you write it?'

'No!' Madhavi shook her head vehemently.

'I don't believe you.' He turned away from her.

There was a moment's hesitation, and then she followed him, and placed a tentative hand on his shoulder.

'Yes, I wrote it. But it wasn't meant for you.'

Uthiyan gritted his teeth. He prised her hand away from his shoulder. 'Then for whom?'

'For your brother. Shenguttuvan.'

Uthiyan inhaled sharply.

'Things got confused. I wrote it for your brother. Your uncle – my patron – Karikala Chola, wanted you on the throne.'

'How did I end up being the one targeted?'

'There are ways of getting a message across to Kaveripattinam quickly. I informed your uncle of the situation and I received a reply asking me to cooperate in a certain scheme to get you on the throne. That was what I thought I was doing. Now I realize there was a double agent somewhere.'

Uthiyan was aghast. 'How can I believe you?'

She spread her arms open in a gesture of entreaty. 'I don't know.'

'It's worse than that. If it hadn't been me, it would have been my brother,' Uthiyan spat out.

Madhavi was silent.

'He will make a better king than I ever would.' He rounded on her in anger. 'Why are you here? Why did you bring me along with you?'

'I thought that was what your uncle would want. For me to keep an eye on you. To keep him apprised of your whereabouts.'

'That's all?'

'No, Uthiyan, I love you!'

'You wish to be a queen,' Uthiyan snapped viciously.

Madhavi shook her head. 'No. That life is not for me.'

'Then why?'

She sighed. 'I owe my king. He is my foremost patron. Without him, I would be nothing. Without his patronage, I don't know what I would be. I shudder to think of it. And so I owe him loyalty.'

'Loyalty!' Uthiyan repeated through gritted teeth. 'Fine words for a courtesan,' he added sarcastically.

'I may be a courtesan, but I know what loyalty is.'

'If you choose your king over me, how can I trust you?'

Madhavi remained silent.

Uthiyan paced back and forth restlessly. 'She's dead. Kannaki. We came here. And now she's dead. We killed her.'

'No, Uthiyan!'

But this is what Uthiyan had been musing on, for the last hour, as the crowd had wept and mourned and shrieked and screamed for their dead queen. It seemed to him that everything had happened because of him. That Kannaki had died as a direct result of events that had been set in motion by his arrival. Then Pekan would have never lusted after Madhavi, nor would he have attempted to gamble for power with

Uthiyan – all of those things that had brewed into the stormy argument between Kannaki and her husband, that Uthiyan had overheard the previous evening . . . perhaps she would not have taken her life.

'If we hadn't come here, she might still be alive. We killed her.'

'Uthiyan,' Madhavi replied, desperate, 'they say that it was an illness that ate into her flesh and caused her pain beyond imagining . . .'

'It wasn't just that, Madhavi. Her husband lusted after you, as he has lusted after other dancers.'

'Don't lay her death at my door! Uthiyan–'

But Uthiyan walked away from her.

She didn't follow him.

25

A white glimmer in the trees. The glinting edge of a knife.

Panic.

A man ahead, shaking in fear. A black shadow against more blackness.

The wide, wide whites of his eyes.

There's something else. Something beyond the trees.

Squealing. The sound of a pig being gutted.

The gurgle of blood.

Silence.

The same dream that tormented him on the ship had returned. Uthiyan woke up on the threadbare mat on the cold floor of the servants' hall. Moonlight glimmered through an open window.

His head was a mess. The assassin's bloodied corpse and the sight of blood spilling out of his open throat had returned to haunt him.

And then Madhavi.

Madhavi, whom he loved but couldn't trust.

Madhavi and Sattan – and Uthiyan felt a pang of jealousy pierce his heart.

The tangled politics of court. Vel Pekan talking of the Kalabhras. He had escaped the intrigues of one court to find another. He thought to flee his family but he found the same demands, the same ties, the same quarrels and rivalries in the shape of his lover and his friend. This time they urged him to wage war on the same family he had left behind.

His thoughts shifted to Kannaki and her red-rimmed, weeping eyes. Her oozing red breast. Her corpse, weighted down by the ornaments and gold of her royal position, floating on the waters of the river that ran past Pekan's palace and through the kingdom of Aykudi.

Why was he born a prince? Why was he the subject of a prophecy?

The fates, surely, had made a mistake with him.

Why was he here?

And then, just like that, he decided to leave. Again.

Book 3

Forest

26

It was all Madhavi's fault.

Three days later, dressed again in the robes of a monk, a begging bowl tied around his waist, his head shaven, that was all Uthiyan could think of, gripping the hilt of his dagger tightly, slashing his way through the forested slopes of Aykudi, as if fighting his way through a battlefield thick with the bodies of imaginary enemies, hacking at Pekan's precious pepper vines with the heat and the anger of a warrior bent on revenge.

It was all Madhavi's fault.

The thought kept repeating, like a mantra in his mind, stoking his rage.

Everything was *her* fault.

If only she hadn't come to Vanchi–

If only he hadn't been besotted with her–

Then soldiers loyal to his brother would have never set upon him–

His mother would have never dared to set out plotting against her husband–

Her husband, in turn, would have had no reason to disown his son–

He would have never accompanied her to Ay, never become a pawn in Pekan's intrigues, and Kannaki, tormented by jealousy and grief, would have never killed herself.

Uthiyan remembered the sight of Kannaki's body, burdened with gold and ornaments, her wet clothes askew and–

The bloody, cancerous wound on her breast.

She would have died anyway, in time, he thought.

No, a voice whispered in his mind, she killed herself. And it was all *your* fault.

'No!' he cried out, startling a bunch of birds in a nearby tree. 'It was not!'

Then whose fault was it?

Madhavi's? Pekan's? The earlier dancing girl who Pekan lusted after? Paranar and Kapilar, for their poems had failed?

The astrologer? The scheming Velir chief who had come to his father's court? His father? His mother?

Who was responsible for Kannaki's death?

Who was guilty?

Were they all guilty?

Or was it him?

Uthiyan stopped and sank to his knees, plunging his dagger into the earth. Him. The one answer that he kept returning to, the truth that strung all of these other answers together into a story that made sense.

What could he do? He looked up at a clear sky unmarred by clouds, a flock of birds flying in formation. Why had the gods and goddesses designed this peculiar fate for him?

He mopped his brow with the dirt-stained edge of his monk's robe. At midday, Uthiyan was faced with a difficult choice. Here, by a river that wound its way around Pekan's mountain, he found a well-trodden path, scuffed by the wheels of carts. He knew, from what he had heard, that turning one way would bring him closer to Puhar, the seat of his uncle Karikala Chola.

There Uthiyan would meet with luxury and safety at the court, but he would also meet Madhavi.

Madhavi, who, no doubt, would have already tried to replace him in her bed. Uthiyan froze. Would Sattan – for he had seen the way his friend had looked at the dancer – would Sattan remember his friend? But how could he say no to such a beautiful woman?

Unbidden, an image of Madhavi and Sattan embracing rose in Uthiyan's mind.

Bile rose in his throat.

No, not Puhar. Not Puhar, where, as well, reason told him, his ambitious, belligerent uncle would seek to play him against his brother and father and inveigle him in games of war.

The other path would take him to Madurai.

Madurai of the famed Sangam.

Legend had it that Brahma had cursed his wife, Goddess Sarasvathi, the goddess of the alphabet, to split herself into as many parts as there were letters of the alphabet, and be reborn in the tongues of forty-eight poets, of different castes and communities. These poets, born in different walks of life, but brought together by their divine skill, gathered at the many-pillared pattimandapam that the Pandyan king had built specially for them – the Sangam. And the god Shiva had himself come down in human form, and taken the ivory-carved seat at the Sangam meant for the forty-ninth poet.

Paranar had told him stories and stories of the Sangam, of the sharp critic Nakkiran and his acerbic tongue. Uthiyan had long fantasized of going to Madurai, to the pattimandapam of Neduncheliyan, and claiming one of the seats meant for the forty-eight prized poets of the Sangam, his poetry famous across Tamilaham.

Is that what he should do?

He picked at his monk's robes, and scratched at his shaven head. He might dream of the Sangam, but in Madurai, in Neduncheliyan's court, even in disguise he would be recognized by someone or the other – even one of the poets, like Paranar – who had visited his father's court.

And then again the intrigues would begin.

It seemed to Uthiyan that the same fate faced him, whichever way he turned.

Which way should he go? What should he do?

Hours later, the sky turned into a shimmering, molten red haze, as if consumed by a slow-moving fire. Uthiyan was still gripped by indecision. Night was poised to arrive soon; already Uthiyan could discern a blue tinge spreading across the edge of the horizon, waiting for the sun to fade away.

Uthiyan sighed. He'd make a choice in the morning. Where would he spend this night? Last night he had a found a cave to sleep in; the night before that a crumbling, abandoned hut.

But now he was in the heart of the fabled forests of

Aykudi, teeming with leopards, tigers and elephants; the beasts whose capture and trade had made Pekan rich. Already, he could hear the bellows, low roars and croaks signalling that the nocturnal creatures of the forest had woken. There was a faint hiss in the tall grass to his left. Uthiyan recoiled. This was not a safe place. Why had he tarried so long?

In the end, he decided that the beasts of the air were safer than those that slither on the ground. He scurried up a nearby tree. There were leopards, he knew, that leapt from branch to branch. But better a leopard, he decided, than a cobra.

It was hard to sleep. At first his robe, stiff with sweat and dirt troubled him, then the rough bark grated his skin. Next, a red ant crawled up and down his arm; then a mosquito settled to feast on him. Finally, he fell asleep, only to jerk awake, terrified by the thought that in his sleep he might roll, slip and fall to the ground. A low growl beneath the tree left him shaking with fear. And as Uthiyan settled again to sleep, it seemed that the flickering stars above, watching him, jested at his fear.

He twisted and turned and finally managed to fall asleep.

~

Uthiyan jolted upright. It felt as if someone or something was watching him.

With a start, Uthiyan turned around. There was something there, hovering above him – the faintest glimmer of eyes – watching him.

Panic seized Uthiyan.

'Who are you?' he croaked, fear gripping his throat.

'I am Death,' came a whisper.

It seemed to Uthiyan that a shadow slithered out from the branch above him, blacker than darkness, blacker than anything he had seen before, a shadow in the shape of a naked woman, with breasts and belly and buttocks. With inhuman, feral grace, the shadow limbered down the tree, monkey-like, to squat at the base of Uthiyan's branch.

Uthiyan scrambled up and away from it, but the branch, thinner as it extended out, bent under his weight. He stopped, paralysed, as the branch swayed dangerously.

'Prince, I am hungry,' the shadow rasped, and inched forward, crawling closer to him.

Uthiyan, his heart beating a tattoo in his chest, managed to shake his head. 'I-I am no prince.'

'But you are.'

His palms sweaty, Uthiyan struggled to grip the branch. 'What do you want from me?'

'I am following you.'

'Why?'

'Didn't the queen tell you? Dharma comes to kings in the shape of death.'

'I am not a king!'

'Ah.' The shadow seemed to shrug. 'A minor detail. What is the difference between a prince and a king? You are a prince who was fated to be a king, and you have chosen to flee your fate, your dharma – whatever you choose to call it. And so you have left me hungry, wanting. What can you give me to sate my hunger?'

There was a burning sensation in Uthiyan's chest, right below his heart, beating fast enough to burst. Squeezing his lungs. It was as if he couldn't breathe.

'That's right, you should be scared, Prince.' The shadow – although there was no way Uthiyan could say how he knew this – smiled. 'Why does Death follow you, again and again and again?'

And with that the shadow was close enough to open its mouth, to reveal a pulsing, blood-red tongue. Uthiyan shrank back, but there was nothing for it – for the mouth grew and grew, bigger and bigger, swallowing everything up – the branch, him, the whole world.

27

Uthiyan awoke, spreadeagled on the same branch that he had fallen asleep on, his head throbbing, as if instead of spending a night tormented by nightmares, he had spent the evening, as he had in times past, finishing a flagon of Yavana wine with Sattan. He shook his head; his dreams last night had been so vivid, that in remembering them he could feel his palms slick with sweat, he could smell, faintly, the acrid, fetid stink that had emanated from the shadow-woman.

He slid down the branches of the tree, and feasted on a clump of nuts that some too-clever squirrel had secreted away by the base of the tree trunk. His head still reeling, he made his way down to where a stream, some offspring or stepdaughter of the Vaigai, cut its way through the forest.

As he submerged his head below the water he heard a faint cry. Startled, he rose, head dripping.

Again he heard something – help, please help.

Not much more than a whisper.

He looked around. There was nobody in sight. Only an immense banyan tree, aeons old, so large that an entire village could live comfortably on it, roots and branches and trunks spreading across the sandy bank and into the stream itself.

'Help me, please!'

He heard the call again, louder, and he looked up into the crowd of branches and hanging roots to discern a small figure crouched up high on a branch above him.

He moved closer, right underneath, and looked up into the face of a young woman – not long out of girlhood, her face wan and tired. As she moved, Uthiyan caught sight of a rotund belly, straining against her skin.

'Help me, please. I am so thirsty. Help me,' she cried weakly.

Uthiyan stared at her, perplexed. 'How did you get up there?'

She motioned for a drink. 'Thirsty, please.'

Uthiyan looked around. There was a small pond,

further back, of lotuses, and he plucked a large lotus leaf, twisted and rolled it into a cone, which he filled with water from the stream. Then carefully, with one hand, he climbed up a hanging root, and handed the leaf to the young woman.

She drank greedily.

He pulled himself on a branch close to her.

'How did you get up here?' He was astonished. Close up, she was even younger than he had first imagined, and heavily pregnant. Her face was wet with tears; she had spent the night, it seemed, crying in the tree.

'There were four of us, heading to Madurai. We were hungry, and we killed one of the wild water buffaloes. I think a tiger smelt the blood, he came that night, and pounced on the corpse. It was frightening. I was terrified. Everyone was screaming. The others ran as fast as they could. I couldn't' – she gestured to her belly – 'run as fast. But the tiger was there right behind me. Somehow, I don't know how, I got myself up this tree. I don't know how I managed it.'

She gulped, and the tears began again. 'But they left me here. It's been a day now, and they haven't come back for me. Adigal,' she said, using the honorific for an ascetic, 'I can't get down.'

It took a long time to convince the young woman to slowly make her way down the branch, to where a prop root grew.

'It's not going to bear my weight, Adigal,' she said, petrified.

'It will.'

'No.' She shook her head vigorously. 'No, it won't.'

Uthiyan, exasperated, sighed. 'I'll be here, nothing will happen to you.'

She looked doubtfully at the root.

Uthiyan tried again. 'I will use all the accumulated power of all my penance to protect you.' He felt deceitful, but it was what he thought was going to get this innocent, believing village girl down the tree.

Her demeanour changed all at once, and she gingerly put out one hand to grasp the root.

'Come on. You can do it.'

She managed, with Uthiyan's coaching, finally to make it down.

As soon as her feet touched the ground she burst into tears.

'I was terrified,' she said, clutching at him, her fingernails digging into his arms. 'I thought I was going to die.'

'It's all right,' he said, patting her awkwardly. She felt too close, he could feel the pressure of her large, taut belly on his stomach – suddenly it felt like her belly had punched him.

Startled, he jumped back, releasing her.

'Oh, the baby, it kicked!' she exclaimed, beginning to giggle, between her tears.

Uthiyan stared at her, puzzled and smiling. 'What is a pregnant woman doing in the forest?'

'I'm on my way to Madurai to join my husband. It's a long story.' She sighed. She looked at him hopefully. 'Will you take me to Madurai?'

'No.' Uthiyan shook his head. 'I can't.'

'Please.'

When Uthiyan remained silent, she crouched down awkwardly, stiff and burdened by the weight of her belly, to kneel at his feet.

'It's not where I'm headed to,' he replied gently, raising her to her feet. 'I'll take you back to your village . . .'

'Please. Please.' She clung to him, her grip fierce and desperate. 'You have to. I have nobody. There's no one in my village to care for me. There's only my husband. And he's in Madurai.'

'I don't know how to get to Madurai.'

'I do!' she exclaimed. 'I know the way. The men in my caravan discussed it – I listened. I know how to get there. But I am too scared to go on my own. I can't go through this forest by myself. Adigal, please, please take pity on me. Please help me.'

Uthiyan sighed. It seemed that despite his best intentions fate was prodding him in this direction.

'Fine, I'll take you to Madurai.'

'Thank you!' She burst into a big smile. 'Thank you! Thank you so much, Adigal!'

Uthiyan felt like an impostor. 'Well, then, what's your name?'

'Kannaki.'

He froze. 'Did you say Kannaki?'

She nodded.

Uthiyan shuddered. Was this merely a coincidence? 'I knew someone else with that name.'

'What was she like?'

'Very different from you.'

28

One poet had compared the cluster of rivulets that flowed into the Vaigai to the curling locks of Lord Shiva. The story was that the god had once called upon Ganga, whom he had trapped in his hair, to descend upon the land of the Pandyas, not long after he had married Princess Meenakshi, in order to sate the thirst of the demon Kundotaran. But Uthiyan found the endless twists and coils of the river reminded him of a writhing mass of serpents, as he attempted to divine, with the help of the directions Kannaki remembered, which branch of the river would lead them to the city of Madurai.

His companion was a source of constant chatter, bubbling with excitement. 'Oh look!' she would exclaim, distracting Uthiyan from his scrutiny of the river, and he would look up – expecting some alarming sight – a tiger – only to be confronted by the sight of a male peacock, his tail feathers spread out, iridescent hues blazing in the morning light.

Her chatter and her exclamations would have caused him much irritation in his previous life. As a prince he would have scorned her country ways and her lack of sophistication but now he was surprised to find himself charmed by her artless, uncontrived manners and endless curiosity. There was something very appealing in her quick, easy smile; so different from the affected, practised simpers that were rife in his mother's court.

She had never been to Madurai, never been out of her hamlet. She pestered and pelted Uthiyan with a thousand questions. Her eyes lit up and grew wide as Uthiyan described the Yavanas he had met in Vanchi, and told her the tales that he had once been told.

Her eyes had widened even further when Uthiyan had described the thousand-pillared pattimandapam of Neduncheliyan, where Shiva took his seat. Or the story of the king who fought in the great war, and demanded an heir – then the great goddess herself chose to be reincarnated as his daughter, Meenakshi, and how she conquered the three realms, even dethroning the king of the devas, Indra.

Kannaki, when she had run out of questions, told him her story. She was born of the Maravar, and–

'The Maravar?' Uthiyan stopped in his tracks.

She nodded. And then a little shyly, added, 'We're not all like what you think.'

Dimly, Uthiyan recalled that the Maravar were robbers who shunned dharma and lived in the forests near Madurai. They were the bane of merchants who used the land routes between Puhar and Madurai, whose caravans and convoys were constantly raided. The Maravar, when found, had died, impaled by the kings of Madurai and Puhar, and these kings had long sought to find the secret home of the Maravar – but with no success.

Uthiyan, surprised, now understood why Kannaki had been so loath for him to take her back home, for they kept the location of their village secret, to avoid capture.

'But why are you heading to Madurai?' he asked, puzzled, for the Maravar – due to their reputation – shunned cities.

Kannaki continued with her story. When she had

turned sixteen, her clansmen had robbed the train of a merchant from Puhar, and taken his son Kovalan – a bright, handsome youth – hostage.

News came back that the merchant had nothing to spare, he had gone bankrupt, there was no money, and he advised the Maravar to keep his good-for-nothing son.

And so Kovalan had languished, fate unknown, frustrated, and Kannaki, the only child of a widowed mother, who had spent her entire life till that point tending her mother's cows, had fallen in love with him, wooed – so Uthiyan gathered – by his tales of city life, awed by his claims of wealth and the manners of a rich man's son.

Soon, she was with child. And so they had been married, and Kovalan – for he was too gentle, too civilized, too bronzed by the city to fit in with the ways of Maravar – had set off to Madurai to make his fortune, and to send for Kannaki when he was established there. He had friends – a merchant and his wife – in Madurai, he had told Kannaki and the Maravar confidently, and they would help him.

A most incongruous couple, concluded Uthiyan, thinking of Kovalan and Kannaki. Kannaki was besotted, but the Kovalan she painted seemed like a risky fellow who didn't truly care for her. A dilettante.

And now, when months later he had not returned, and Kannaki, despite the advice of her kinsmen, had got tired of her mother's cows and had bravely chosen to set off for Madurai.

When twilight fell they chose a sheltered spot by the river to rest. 'Sing me a song,' Uthiyan, who delighted in music, pleaded. 'Sing me a song that your people sing.'

'Only if you will tell me a story, Adigal!' she quipped in return.

He agreed, and she sang for him the song of the Kuruvai dance, the song that lovelorn cow girls sang as they minded their cattle, waiting for love to somehow, in the midst of their dreary boredom, strike them.

> Friend! Mayavan swung a stone, and knocked down
> all the orchard's fruit.
> If he came down to see our herd, then we would
> hear the lovely sound
> of his most wondrous flute.
>
> Friends, Mayavan churned the ocean,
> using a snake for rope.

If he came down to tend our herd,
then we could enjoy the sound
of his long bamboo flute.

Friends! Mayavan tore up the wild citrus tree
that stood in our vast pastureland.
Should he appear amidst our herd,
then we should have a chance to hear
his sweet shepherd's flute.

Let's sing now of the bewitching loveliness
of Pinnai, who is dancing near the river
with the boy she loves so tenderly.

How can we describe his magic
when he hid the garments of the girls
whose waists appeared so fragile
that, bending, they might have broken?

How can we describe the face
of the lovely girl distressed by the remorse
of him who stole her dress?

How can we describe the loveliness
of her who stole the heart of him
who loved her but fooled her like the other women
while they were playing in the stream?

How can our words express the charm
of him who took the favours and the rings
of her who stole his heart?

How can we picture the sweet face
she hid behind her lovely hands
when he had stolen her garments and her jewels?

And how can we describe the grace
of his repentance when he saw
with what distress
she hid the fairness of her face
within the darkness of her hands?

And this had happened to Kannaki. He stared at her moon-shaped face, illuminated by the ruddy glow of the fire she had just started, as she sang. Something tugged at his heart. She was entirely unlike the sophisticated, coiffed women he had known, but at that moment – her song, the twilight, the wisps of hair that darted around her pretty, fire-brightened face – he felt he was in the presence of true beauty.

So different from Madhavi.

Kannaki, as if sensing his thoughts, looked up and caught him watching her. The song died on her lips. 'What,' she said, self-consciously, 'what are you looking at?'

'Nothing.' He rose then, to put out the fire.

'What about my story?' she demanded.

'Tomorrow night,' he replied. 'We are still at least two days from Madurai, and we'll need all our strength for the morrow.'

29

The next night she persisted until he agreed to tell her a story.

'What sort of story would you like?' Uthiyan asked.

To his surprise, she did not want a tale of kings or princes or princesses, of battlefields or grand marriages.

'Then what kind of story do you want?'

'I don't know.' She shrugged. 'Something different. Stories always seem to happen to princes or kings, or gods or goddesses. Isn't there anything about normal people?' She twisted a coil of hair around her finger. 'Don't stories or adventures happen to normal people?'

Uthiyan rattled the contents of his memory, and all he could come up with was a half-remembered tale that the poet Nathakuthanaar had sung, a long time ago, at his father's court.

Once upon a time, a long, long time ago, there lived in the city of Kasi a wondrously beautiful courtesan. So accomplished was she, so skilled and talented, intelligent and exquisite, versed in all the sixty-four arts, that she commanded a great fee – a few thousand gold pieces for a night. Rich men from all across the world would journey to Kasi for a glimpse of her and a chance at securing her favours.

Until one day.

Until one day when she caught sight of, from a window, a thief about to be hanged. This thief was a strong and handsome man, with well-muscled arms that, rumour had it, had once brought down an elephant. He had used his strength to great effect in robbing the citizens of Kasi. Now, he had been caught and was about to die.

The courtesan fell in love with the thief.

She begged and she pleaded for his life, and when that had no effect, she bought his life for a great fortune and made the dispensers of justice rich.

For a few months, all was well. The courtesan bid her paramours and admirers farewell and devoted herself solely to the love of the man whose life she had saved.

Until one day.

Until one day, the thief, as was his wont and is often the wont of men who find themselves in situations that they do not deserve and have achieved without great striving, got restless. He wished to leave Kasi, he was bored, his fingers twitched for the excitement of a caper, a theft, a robbery. Although he was surrounded by the great wealth of his wife, it galled him that all this belonged to her, and not truly to him – even though the courtesan, so besotted was she, would have given it all to her husband had he but asked.

So what did the thief do? It was not enough for him merely to leave. No, for he desired the wealth of his wife, worth hundreds of thousands of gold pieces.

The thief hatched a plan. He would command her to put on her best and finest ornaments to visit the shrine of a deity just beyond the city, situated on a high hill. Once there, he would coax her to remove her ornaments and then push her off the hill. The drop would kill her, and the thief would be free to abscond with all her wealth.

And so, the thief persuaded his wife to do exactly as he wished – claiming that this deity had in fact saved his life, and he owed the deity prayers and oblations. The courtesan, following the instructions of her husband, dressed herself in her finest garments, anointed herself with the most expensive scents and perfumes, and wore the grandest, most expensive ornaments she possessed.

Together, clasping hands, they climbed the great hill to reach the shrine.

There, the thief instructed his wife to remove her priceless jewels.

'But why?' the courtesan asked.

'I am going to kill you,' the thief replied. 'But I must have your jewels first.'

Surprise, grief, rage, shock, anger all vied for the courtesan's attention. What should she do? What could she do? Her husband was far stronger than he was. She was desperate. She was about to lose her life to a man she loved.

And then, something strange happened. Something that words cannot entirely explain. She removed her ornaments as instructed, and, with all the demure humility that she could muster, she approached her husband.

'I have done as you wished, as a good wife should obey the command of her husband,' she whispered. 'But grant me one last favour. I have loved you with all my heart, let me love you, this one last time, before I go to my death.'

The thief assented. It seemed like a harmless

request, and what fault could he find with it? And like many men, he would not say no to a last bout of lovemaking with a beautiful woman. So he let his wife approach him, and let her put her arms around him.

With superhuman strength she grabbed him by his hinder parts, and flung him off the hill.

The thief tumbled to his death, his wife watching.

A miracle had just happened, magical strength had been granted for that one instant to the courtesan, and her life had been saved. For that one instant, she had been possessed by the goddess, she had become the goddess – Aiyai, Durga, Kuttuvai.

She left her ornaments on that hill, and walked down, alone. What happened – in that moment between thought and action – had changed the courtesan forever. What happened cannot be explained. But in that instant, forced with the prospect of death, when the courtesan asked for divine aid, and was possessed with the strength of the goddess, she was awarded a glimpse of all life, of the universe, of all the truths that sages spend years in penance to acquire, of the true nature of reality, of who she truly was and who we all are. She was awakened. She was enlightened.

She came down the hill, and gave away all her wealth. She cut her beautiful hair and took on the robes of an ascetic. She spent the rest of her life with a begging bowl in hand, bringing the knowledge of what was revealed to her in that moment to all. She became a great teacher. Some say her name was Sulaza. Others claim that it was Bhadra. And after her transformation, she was known as Kundalakesi – the one with short, curly locks.

'Kundalakesi,' Kannaki murmured. 'That's a nice name.' She caressed her belly. 'Perhaps if my baby is a girl, I will call her that. But–' she frowned now – 'I don't know if Kovalan would like that.'

'Why?'

'Manimekalai, the goddess of the seas, is his family deity – he told me he was descended from her!'

Uthiyan turned over, and closed his eyes. He was just about to slip off into slumber, when Kannaki asked, 'What about your family?'

Uthiyan stifled a groan and tried to feign sleep.

'Don't you have a family?'

Uthiyan gave up and replied, 'Yes, I do. I have a mother, brother and father.'

'Don't you miss them?'

Uthiyan gazed up at the stars. 'Yes. Sometimes.'

Kannaki propped herself up on one elbow to squint at him. 'Why did you leave them?'

How could he explain, how could he tell of her all

that had happened in Vanchi, at this father's court? It was mere months ago, but now it seemed like another life. How could he tell her of his mother's ambitions, the muddle with his brother, the astrologer's prophecy, or how his own father had betrayed him?

'You come from a rich family. I can tell by the way you speak, your mannerisms. You don't come from people like me. If I had wealth, I can't imagine begging for meals and owning just one garment!'

Uthiyan let out an exasperated groan.

Kannaki persisted. 'What made you choose this life of an ascetic, begging for meals?'

Uthiyan sighed. He couldn't tell her the truth, but he supposed he could invent a story that resembled the truth. 'My father was a merchant, and then one day he lost a great deal of wealth when one ship was lost at sea.' He paused, realizing that he was borrowing from Madhavi's story. 'There wasn't enough of a portion left for two sons. So I gave up my claim, leaving what remained of the business to my brother and took up the robes of a monk instead.'

'Have you seen them since?'

Uthiyan shook his head.

'Don't you miss your mother?'

'Yes.'

Kannaki was silent. Uthiyan looked at her after a

while – surprised by this unusually long silence. She was asleep.

But sleep eluded Uthiyan. He found himself thinking of his mother. She must have thought of him often. Would she be lonely in her Silver Palace, he wondered? Would she have fought with his father?

His father. Uthiyan didn't imagine that his father thought of him often.

But it was his brother on whom his mind lingered. He wondered how Shenguttuvan was faring now, for he had heard that Shenguttuvan had fought with their father. He hadn't had time to say farewell to his brother. He wished he had been able to. They had left things in such a messy tangle between them. The astrologer's prophecy, the business with Venmal, his father playing them off against each other – those last few days in Vanchi had been so fraught. He longed to have been able to tell his brother that he believed he would be a good king, that he had nothing but love for him. That no matter what any astrologer said or what the courtiers believed – Uthiyan would not have stolen his brother's destiny.

He missed his brother.

The next day, they reached Madurai.

30

The procession that passed them by on the road to Madurai took Kannaki's breath away. She stood there gaping, Uthiyan observed, in the dust kicked up by the hordes of richly caparisoned elephants, chariots and horses. She seemed stunned by the appearance of the Pandyan crown prince, dressed in gleaming armour in the Yavana style. It shone like gold, dazzling in the light of the noonday sun. He was mounted on an elephant adorned with golden ornaments. She gawked at the warriors who followed in his wake, some on horses, others on foot, bearing gleaming spears, lances and swords.

And after the army passed by, a retinue of dancing girls, clowns and musicians followed – all intended to entertain the Komahan as he travelled.

Kannaki's eyes grew wider and wider as she took in the size and extravagance of this procession. She pulled at Uthiyan's arm to catch his attention. 'Where are they going?'

Uthiyan was about to say that he did not know, but a man piloting a heavily loaded luggage wagon in the army's wake caught Kannaki's question. 'To Korkai!'

'Why?'

'The king sends his son and his army to fight the Kalabhras, who sport themselves in our lands near Korkai, stealing our cattle!' the man thundered back.

Not just cattle, it must also be pearls; Uthiyan recalled that all the famous pearls of the Pandyas came from Korkai, pearls that made their way to Yavana lands at exorbitant prices – the source of Madurai's wealth and glory. If the Kalabhras sought to wrest control of these fisheries, they would stop the flow of Yavana gold into Pandyan coffers.

This could change everything.

The Kalabhras. Uthiyan's mind raced back to Aykudi, to all those conversations with Vel Pekan about the movements of the Kalabhras, and their ambitions to wage war on the Pandyas. Pekan had tried to divert their attention to take on the Cheras, and had hoped to inveigle him into this plot. Uthiyan breathed a sigh of relief that it hadn't come to pass. But he frowned, remembering Paranar's words and the sight of the lean, lithe Kalabhras encampment that Pekan had taken him to – the Kalabhras were unlike anything that Tamilaham had seen, and that they would change the land forever.

But could the Kalabhras take the city of Madurai? Uthiyan had no doubt that they could cause trouble in Korkai or another Pandyan town or village, but he knew – from all the lessons at court – that Madurai was close to impregnable and the Pandyas were fierce warriors. King Neduncheliyan lavished rich rewards on the poets of his famous Sangam, to sing praises of his victories and prowess on the battlefield, so that these songs travelled even further, further than any spear or arrow could reach, to strike fear in the hearts of his enemies and their armies.

Moreover, the city was fortified – by an unbroken wall that began at Karur, the place where the realms of the three crowned kings of Tamilaham met, ranged across the plains and the hills to encircle the city of Madurai and the shrine of the goddess Meenakshi.

The city itself boasted of even greater defence measures that Uthiyan could see as he and Kannaki approached the city. Water diverted from the Vaigai was drawn into channels to form a moat girdling the city walls, which the Pandyas kept richly stocked with crocodiles, to fend off all besiegers and attackers.

The city itself, within its walls, was cruelly hot. Wilting under the burning sun, slender-waisted maidens attired in the finest silks, furiously fanned themselves. Kannaki, though she was exhausted after the long trip, could not help staring at the fine diamonds, emeralds and intricate gold ornaments that these maidens sported.

She was fascinated by their hairstyles, Uthiyan noticed. Some women had their hair piled in numerous buns, others had pinned it to one side, and still others had it in plaits fastened to the back, fixed with golden chains, studded with pearls and flowers of different hues. Kannaki ogled at the attire of these maidens – brocaded silks, long lengths of coral and pearls, shoulder bangles and arm bangles, bracelets at the wrist and lengths of gold across slim waists, a profusion of anklets clattering and clinking as they walked, earrings so heavy that ear lobes gaped. They were draped in brocaded cloth and silk, and their mulaikaccus were made of cloth, or covered in pearls and fastened as bodices.

She stared, an unmistakable country bumpkin, and the maidens tittered back, all city hauteur, hiding their disdainful smiles underneath their fans. Uthiyan squirmed, embarrassed, and urged a reluctant Kannaki along the streets. It was hard work, for there were streets filled with wonders that arrested Kannaki's attention. There was one with only jewellers, another where courtesans lived, and – Uthiyan could not think of anything more boring – a street for grain merchants.

He lead Kannaki past shimmering pools of red and purple lotuses and heaps of jasmine and kurinji flowers in the marketplace. They passed by pearls from Korkai, still smelling of oysters, under gem-encrusted canopies that stretched out to provide shade from the sun. The gardens of Madurai, teeming with elephants, and birds of great variety, were like nothing Kannaki had ever seen.

Soon they came across the elegant, palatial homes of the merchants' quarter. Carved elephants held aloft a gilded roof; a frieze of prancing horses provided the balustrade for a veranda; plumed peacocks chased each other along the length of a staircase.

Kannaki's eyes lit up at the sight of these finely chiselled balconies, ornamented with exquisitely etched statues and painted in rich colours. Did Kovalan's friends live in a home like this?

But their name elicited no recognition. They tried at all the houses, Kannaki's face growing dimmer and dimmer as the hours wore by. Until, finally they met an old man who recalled the name. Yes, the name was familiar. But the merchant had died years ago, and now his wife, the old man believed, lived in a distant quarter, a suburb of the city. He gave them directions.

Following his directions, they reached the suburb, a far cry from the mansions of the rich they had seen earlier. They finally arrived at their destination – a home just off the main street. A modest place, nothing like the mansions that Kannaki's imagination had conjured.

Nonetheless, she was breathless with excitement. She was going to see Kovalan.

A grey-haired woman, clad in a green silk garment, was sitting on the parapet outside the house. Kannaki brightly introduced herself as Kovalan's wife. The woman listened, and looked Kannaki up and down. Kannaki, self-conscious, tried to neaten her travel-stained and creased garments. The woman's expression was veiled, but Uthiyan could sense just the slightest bit of contempt. She had the airs of a sophisticated, rich city woman – but looking at her home, Uthiyan knew those days were behind her. She stared at Kannaki's pregnant belly. But, it seemed to Uthiyan, with a slight reluctance, she led them into the house.

'Where is Kovalan?' Kannaki asked politely, as they entered.

'He has gone out, but he will be back soon,' the woman – Madari, her name was – replied.

Uthiyan rose to leave, but Kannaki requested that he stay to meet Kovalan.

The time seemed to stretch. Uthiyan was uneasy – this situation, of Madari and her contempt of Kannaki's village ways, did not bode well. He rose again, but just at that moment Kovalan arrived.

He was young and handsome – everything that Uthiyan had expected. But he had a disgruntled air about him.

Kannaki's face lit up as he entered the room.

He was surprised to see her. 'Kannaki!'

Kannaki got up to greet him, excited, exuberant.

'How did you get here?' He was astonished.

Kannaki broke into a breathless account of all her adventures – the caravan in the forest, the attack by the tiger, meeting Uthiyan, and she went on. Uthiyan observed Kovalan. Kannaki's husband listened to her, but his mind was elsewhere.

It was almost as if he wasn't too happy by her presence, Uthiyan thought.

Kannaki eventually finished her story and enquired how Kovalan was.

'I am well.' Kovalan sighed heavily. 'But things could be better. There is no work, nothing has come to fruition. The king is, well' – he waved vaguely in the air – 'not concerned about the situation in the city. It is a difficult time. The Kalabhras, they say, are marching towards Pandyan lands.'

Kannaki, now anxious, sat down and played with the edge of her garment. 'What about your father?'

Kovalan hung his head. 'He will have nothing to do with me.' He sighed again.

Uthiyan stood up. The couple clearly had other things to discuss.

Kannaki looked up, realizing for the first time since Kovalan had returned, that Uthiyan was still there. 'Kovalan, this is the ascetic who brought me to Madurai–'

'I have heard much about you, Kovalan, and I am glad to have met you,' Uthiyan interjected. 'There's a monastery outside the town, in the Samanar hills. Now that I have delivered Kannaki into your hands,

I will make my way there.' Uthiyan had heard about the monastery while they were searching for Kovalan's address.

'Please stay, why don't you?' Kannaki pleaded.

Uthiyan refused. Kovalan seemed petulant to him, entitled – it dawned on Uthiyan that he was looking at himself, a distant reflection of himself. Had he been like that in Vanchi? It was an uncomfortable thought.

A few feet from the house, Uthiyan stopped and put a hand to his waist. He could feel it – underneath his robes. It was a dagger, but with a gold hilt, embellished with pearls in the shape of the Chera bow and arrow. Such a thing was of little value in the palace, but to these two, with no income and a child on the way, perhaps it would be of some help.

What use had a monk for a dagger anyway?

He retraced his steps and knocked on the door. This time Kovalan answered.

He handed the dagger over. 'This belonged to me, before I was a monk. I have no use for it now, perhaps it will help you.'

Kovalan's eyes lit up as he looked at it. 'You were once wealthy.'

'Once,' Uthiyan responded. 'But no longer.' He gestured to his robes of bark cloth. 'This is who I am.'

Kovalan bowed. 'Thank you, Adigal. My wife and I are grateful.'

Uthiyan nodded.

'Will you come back to bless the child when it is born?'

Uthiyan, surprised again, found himself agreeing.

31

That night Uthiyan slept on the porch of a small house owned by an old woman. She had begged him to sleep on her bed, believing this would grant her good karma. However, Uthiyan could not help but notice that she moved with difficulty. He had demurred, settling for a spot on her porch where he could stare up at the night sky.

Struggling to fall asleep, he found himself thinking of Kovalan. Had he been like that – privileged, pampered, spoilt?

And yet, unlike Kovalan, Uthiyan had little desire to return home, to the Chera court. It had once seemed to him like the most important place to be in the world. Yet – and Uthiyan could not deny this – he had been bored and restless. These last few months had been completely unexpected, and frightening, but for the first time Uthiyan felt alive. Truly alive. He had come all the way to Madurai, through Vel Pekan's forest, on his own!

And tomorrow he would visit the place that he had dreamt of for so many years – Neduncheliyan's pattimandapam where the poets of the Sangam took their seats.

32

Uthiyan rose, eager, with the dawn. After taking leave of his host, he walked through the city with one goal in mind. When he finally set his eyes upon the famed pattimandapam, painted silver like his mother's palace, blazing with the summer's heat, his heart soared.

This was the gathering place of the finest poets of Tamilaham.

Should he dare present his own poetry here? It was something that he had fantasized about in Vanchi, dreaming up a life where he was a poet like Paranar and Kapilar. But now, now that the object of his fantasies was there, right in front of him, his dreams felt childish. He plucked at his robes. Could a man dressed as a monk venture there and recite poems about love?

They would all laugh at him!

And worse, some of those poets would recognize him, those who had visited his father's court.

No, he could not enter the place. Uthiyan felt his shoulders droop and his heart sink. He lingered there for hours, gazing at the pattimandapam, shining with the lustre of a thousand suns. It was close to noon when he took one last look and turned away. His stomach growled, and he ventured back into the marketplace, hoping to get a meal.

As he went about with his begging bowl in hand, Uthiyan could not help but overhear the rumours coursing through the marketplace. A serving girl whispered to a flower seller the real story behind the Komahan's quick departure to Korkai with the army – it had more to do with a quarrel between the king and the queen than with any actual threat.

Much like Uthiyan, the flower seller was astonished. 'Why?'

A dancing girl, the serving girl claimed, had caught the king's eye and favour. The queen, noticing this, had picked a fight with her husband in front of the whole court. Incensed, the king had responded by withholding a pair of anklets he had ordered from the jeweller for his wife and gifted it to the dancing girl instead.

'The queen must have been furious!' the flower seller exclaimed.

'Of course she was,' the serving girl replied, as Uthiyan continued to eavesdrop. 'She flounced out of court, and half the court scurried behind her. There was mayhem. She locked herself in her apartments, and sobbing. That's what I heard, and she sent for her son, the Komahan.'

'What did she expect him to do?'

'To intervene with the king, silly! But before the Komahan could open his mouth the king ordered him off to Korkai with the army, for news had just come in about the Kalabhras army sporting themselves on our lands!'

Uthiyan turned away. The government of every court in Tamilaham resembled a family quarrel. Everywhere he went it was the same story. Madurai, Aykudi – in every court there seemed to be some dancing girl who attracted the attention of the king. Every court featured a king and a queen at odds with each other, warring through their children. It was the same tale, the same story, everywhere.

Finally, a middle-aged grain merchant invited Uthiyan into his shop and poured rice into his begging bowl. As he did so, the merchant asked, 'Venerable one, where are you from?

Where should he say he was from? His accent would mark him as an outsider. He thought fast. 'From Aykudi.'

The grain merchant smiled. 'What do you think of our city?'

'Beautiful beyond imagination,' Uthiyan replied.

As Uthiyan spoke, a boy ran into the shop, panting as if he had run for miles. The merchant grabbed him by the edge of his lower garment, wrapped and tucked between his thighs. 'You rascal, where have you been?'

'Sir!' The boy was heaving with excitement. 'There's to be an execution this evening, at sundown!'

'What!'

'They caught a murderer!' he replied, with a boy's relish for the most gruesome details.

The merchant gave the boy's head a tap. 'Speak properly in front of a holy man,' he said, gesturing to Uthiyan.

The boy noticed Uthiyan for the first time, and now looked contrite.

Uthiyan laughed. 'Go on,' he said, joining the conversation. 'What happened?'

This galvanized the boy. 'Sir, he murdered someone important. And they're going to cut off his head!'

'Who is he? Someone from Madurai?' the merchant asked.

The boy shook his head. 'No. He's from that tribe, the ferocious one.'

A sense of unease began to stir through Uthiyan. He stared intently at the boy. 'Which tribe?'

The boy frowned, trying to remember. 'What was their name? I can't recall.'

'Try.'

The grain merchant shook his head. 'He can't remember anything! I don't know why I keep him.'

'No, I can remember!' the boy protested. 'I've got it! I remember!' He turned to Uthiyan, triumphantly. 'It's the Eyinar Maravar. That fierce tribe who kill all their enemies.'

Uthiyan's mouth went dry. 'What is the man's name? Do you remember?'

The boy nodded. 'His name is Kovalan.'

Uthiyan felt his heart and his breath stop. 'Excuse me,' he muttered, blundering past the merchant, back on to the street.

33

Kannaki's face was wet with tears, and her long, beautiful hair had come undone. Her clothes were in disarray and she lay on the ground, fists clenched, weeping as if her heart would break.

'She's been like this ever since the news came,' Kovalan's friend, Madari, told him.

At the sound of her voice, Kannaki rose, and turned to see Uthiyan.

'You!' she screamed. 'It's your fault! *You* killed him, and you've pinned it on my poor, innocent husband!'

'What happened?'

'The dagger – the dagger you gave Kovalan, it was used to kill a Chera prince–'

'Child!' Madari scolded. 'This is an ascetic, a holy man – you shouldn't dare, he must have just found it in the forest–'

Uthiyan silenced her with a wave of his hand. He knelt down to face Kannaki. 'What happened?'

'That dagger. It had a bow and arrow symbol – the Chera insignia . . .' Kannaki burst into sobs.

'It was too valuable, with all the pearls and rubies, to belong to anyone less than a prince,' Madari continued, 'so the armourer in the marketplace deemed. He thought that Kovalan had stolen it – how else could he have come into possession of it? He alerted the palace guards, who arrested Kovalan. A Chera prince has been missing, and they think Kovalan killed him. So he will be executed this evening.'

'What?' Uthiyan was stunned. 'Just like that? With no evidence?'

'The king has decreed it. What can we do?' the old woman said.

'Did you kill the prince?' Kannaki, wiping her tears, rose up to face Kovalan. 'You must have.'

'No, I didn't. He is still alive.'

'Where is he then?' Kannaki spat out.

Uthiyan took a deep breath. What should he do? He could not let an innocent man die. But what could he do? If he spoke, if he revealed the truth – it would start all over again.

The blood, the plots, the conspiracy.

The running.

The assassination attempts.

All of it.

He shuddered. 'I'm going to the palace. I'll tell them where the prince is.'

~

Uthiyan stared at the long line of petitioners outside the palace. This was going to take a long time. Hours perhaps. He looked at Kannaki, sweating heavily, breathing hard – the toil of her recent journey and now this news showing in the exhausted slump of her shoulders, her wan face. She shouldn't be here.

He cursed himself.

What had possessed him to give his dagger to Kovalan? It had seemed the right thing at the time, a generous act. What had it led to?

There was a slight commotion along the line of petitioners ahead of him exclaiming and whispering. Kannaki turned and her mouth fell open. She tugged at Uthiyan's garment. 'Who is that?'

'Who?'

Kannaki gestured ahead to the source of the commotion – a beautiful woman dressed in a white gold-bordered mulaikaccu, with a gold and emerald necklace that hung all the way to her waist.

Uthiyan's breath stopped.

It was Madhavi.

'Who is she?' Kannaki repeated, and this time the man standing in front of them turned to answer.

'She's the dancing girl Madhavi, from Puhar. She had come here to entertain the king,' the man whispered.

Another woman standing behind them had heard the whole story from a palace maid. The king had ordered a pair of anklets to be made to please the queen, but when these anklets had arrived, instead of presenting them to his wife, he had given them to this dancing girl, who had complained that she had lost a priceless anklet and that its loss marred her performance. The queen had taken offence and stormed off to her apartments, barring entry to the king and leaving the court in a uproar.

It was the same tale, with a few subtractions and additions, that Uthiyan had heard at the marketplace. Only he hadn't known that the dancing girl was Madhavi, and the anklet was the one he had stolen.

'And now nothing is getting done in the palace,' the woman continued, 'with the courtiers divided into camps. The king has retired from court, and has left all business to his amaiccars.'

The man clucked disapprovingly. 'That is not how a king should rule.'

'Are you all right?' This was Kannaki. Uthiyan felt queasy, his knees were buckling, he felt feverish.

He pulled himself together. 'I'm – I'm fine.'

His head spun, it felt like the walls around him seemed to shift and come closer.

Fate had followed him here too, in the shape of Madhavi and her missing anklet.

All the chaos that he had sought to leave behind had caught up with him.

34

The line shifted and moved and muttered.

Uthiyan gazed at the hall around them. It was much like his father's hall in Vanchi, but here the pillars boasted of emblems that recalled the story of the Pandyas' divine ruler – Goddess Meenakshi. One pillar sported the image of the goddess as a young girl, with the three breasts that had caused great consternation to her father as she emerged from the sacrificial fire of the yagna he had organized to pray for a male heir. Instead he had been bestowed with a three-year-old daughter, with an incredible deformity – three breasts. Astounded, the king had turned to the heavens, asking what he was to do with such a child. How would a three-breasted female freak rule the Pandya lands?

Legend had it that a voice from the heavens had

spoken in response to the king's fevered entreaty, ordering him to raise his daughter as a son, a prince born to rule. And that in time, when his daughter met the one destined to be her husband – her deformity would be healed.

Apart from the deformity, the child was beautiful, with large, expressive eyes, and was named Meenakshi, 'the one with eyes shaped like a fish', inspiring the insignia of the Pandyas – twin fishes that recalled their queen goddess.

Meenakshi had grown up to be an unsurpassed warrior, conquering the three worlds and striking fear in the hearts of all other kings, even the king of the devas, Indra, whose own story was deeply tied up with the origin of the Pandyas and Madurai. Generations earlier, having been cursed after the death of the demon Vritra, Indra had gone into hiding. In the course of his exile, he passed through a grove of kadamba trees, where he found a linga. Indra had worshipped the linga and built a shrine there. A merchant passing by discovered the shrine and informed Kulasekara, then king of the Pandyas, of this mysterious shrine, and Kulasekara, devoted to Shiva, had built a magnificent temple in the grove and relocated his capital.

So Madurai had come to be.

The kadamba trees still grew there, in the temple. Somewhere, within the walls of the palace, was a tree that had been taken as a sapling from the sacred grove. Now, aeons old, it was sacred to the Pandyas, the life force, the spirit, the living embodiment of their dynasty.

It was Kulasekara's son who was the father of Meenakshi, and as this divinely born queen stormed all the realms, Indra sought again the help of Shiva. Meenakshi came to battle with Shiva himself, seeking to conquer Mount Kailasa, and Shiva came to fight in the form of Sundareshwara – the beautiful god. Meenakshi took one look at him, and fell in love. Her third breast disappeared, and instead of a battle, a marriage ensued, with Shiva coming to live with Meenakshi in the temple that her ancestor had built for him.

All of the motifs of the story – the kadamba tree, Indra's battle with Vritra, the merchant stumbling upon the shrine, Kulasekara Pandya moving the Pandya capital to Madurai, the romance between Shiva and Meenakshi, the demon Kundotaran and his insatiable thirst, Ganga transforming herself into Vaigai – were inscribed on the pillars that lined this great hall. As the petitioners moved through the hall, towards the dais, they walked past the story of the divine origins of the Pandyas, the story of Madurai itself.

In a hall much like this, except that the story it told was different, Uthiyan's father sat and administered justice. Uthiyan could not help but think back to the day that his father had sent for him at dawn, to hear petitions. He remembered that line, much like this one, thronging, sweating, coiling down the steps and the palace gardens. On that occasion he had sat inside the hall, by the throne, half-asleep as countless men and women came and lay bare the problems on which their lives and livelihoods depended.

It seemed to Uthiyan a strange quirk of fate now to be in such a line himself, desperate for justice.

Was this another form of justice that fate had concocted for him?

But the line was achingly long. If his turn didn't come before evening fell, Kovalan would be executed. Would their case be heard in time?

Reprieve came in the form of a guard, who noticing Uthiyan's garb and Kannaki's pregnant state, had waved them to the head of the line. Uthiyan offered up a silent prayer of gratitude.

Soon he and Kannaki stood before the king's minister, seated on a stool before the king's throne. The throne itself was empty. The king was elsewhere.

The amaiccar rubbed his bleary eyes and looked at Uthiyan. 'How can I help you, venerable one?'

'This is regarding Kovalan, who has been decreed to be executed for the murder of Prince Uthiyan Cheral.'

'Yes. What of it?'

'I know where the prince is.'

He had the minister's attention now. The amaiccar scrutinized him intently. 'We have sent an olai to the Cheras to inform them that we have apprehended the murderer of their prince. And soon we shall send them the murderer's head. But you say that he isn't dead. So where is he?'

Uthiyan took a deep breath. 'I am the prince.'

The minister cocked an eyebrow. 'You, sir?' His tone was perfectly polite, but Uthiyan could not miss the faint tinge of sarcasm that laced his words.

The crowd behind him tittered. Uthiyan could faintly hear someone exclaim mockingly: 'He thinks he's a prince!'

The words seemed to echo and bounce off the pillars of the gigantic hall. Uthiyan's ears burned. This was not how he had imagined it would go. He had thought that all he had to do was present himself, explain who he was, and they would believe him.

Kannaki looked at him, her face trusting and innocent, her eyes wide with surprise.

He could see the thoughts running through her head.

His manners, his knowledge, the stories he had told her, his education – he could see her reviewing each moment of the acquaintance, and adding it up – and yes, she believed him.

She believed him.

Uthiyan took heart. 'Yes, I *am* the prince.'

The minister crossed his arms and examined Uthiyan again. 'And this garment – this monk's raiment – am I supposed to understand that this is a disguise?'

Uthiyan had reached the end of his patience. 'I have been on the run for months, from assassins out to murder me so that my brother may inherit the throne. So, yes, it *is* a disguise.'

'Hmm.' The minister pondered this. 'Exactly how can you prove this? Anyone can come in here and pretend to be a dead prince to get his friend, a murderer, off the hook. And an ascetic is worthy of respect – but you, by your admission, are not a real one. How can you prove this?'

Who could Uthiyan ask to vouch for him? What would it take to convince this minister? Would there be a poet in the Sangam who would recognize him? Would there be a duta in attendance at the Pandya court, an emissary from the Cheras? But how close would they have come to the Prince Uthiyan Cheral? Would they recognize him stripped of his rich robes and jewellery?

There was only one person he could think of, who was in Madurai, who could definitively identify him.

'Summon the courtesan Madhavi, she was recently at the Chera capital. She knows what the prince looks like.'

'Very well,' the minister said and turned to the herald beside him. 'Summon the dancer Madhavi, and ask the king if he will grant us an audience for this matter.'

The herald bolted. A hush fell on the hall. Uthiyan felt the pressure of a thousand stares boring into his flesh.

He closed his eyes.

35

A herald escorted Uthiyan and Kannaki down a series of corridors. The amaiccar walked ahead of them, surrounded by his retinue of palace guards. The palace seemed endless and Kannaki was clearly nervous; she gripped Uthiyan's hand tight. She was a village girl who had never expected her life to lead her to befriend a prince or to the private quarters and an audience with the Pandya king.

They stopped by a pair of carved wooden doors, painted in gold and silver, and engraved with motifs of the Pandya emblem.

The doors were opened, and Uthiyan heard the unmistakable sound of a woman's laughter.

His pulse quickened. Was it Madhavi? Was she dallying with the Pandya king?

A fire seemed to erupt within him.

The woman laughed again. No, it wasn't her. He exhaled, relieved.

The herald guided them through a series of antechambers, until they reached a large room that boasted of a beautifully wrought couch. On it lay sprawled the king, Neduncheliyan, his garments in disarray.

Uthiyan looked at him in shock. This was not how he had imagined Neduncheliyan, after hearing so much of his battle feats. The corpulent man that lounged on the couch, a golden goblet of Yavana wine held absently between his pudgy fingers, his face swollen and eyes sunken, bore little resemblance to the reputed warrior the poets sang of.

'Come here.' The king crooked a finger and beckoned a beautiful young woman, clad in azure silk, who was tittering at the other end of the room, half-hiding herself behind a wooden column.

The young woman shook her head and laughed.

Neduncheliyan made as if to raise himself off the couch and lunge at her, but just at that moment the minister cleared his throat.

The king turned his head towards the amaiccar, and the small party by the entrance. 'Aah. Is this about the Chera prince?'

'Yes sir' – the minister pointed to Uthiyan with one hand – 'this is him.'

Neduncheliyan hoisted himself to a sitting position. 'If this is him,' he slurred, 'does he know that I bested his father once?'

He turned to Uthiyan. 'And your uncle.'

Uthiyan was silent. The golden goblet was held precariously in the king's hands, and droplets of wine had now began to speckle the king's silk garments.

'Hmph,' the Neduncheliyan mumbled, 'if you were a real Chera, you would have your hand on your sword, and the sword out of its scabbard at that!'

It slowly dawned on Uthiyan that the king was drunk.

'Ko, you sent for me?'

It was Madhavi entering the king's chambers. She was about to kneel before Neduncheliyan when she saw Uthiyan and froze.

'Madhavi!' The king brightened. 'Did you like the anklets?'

Madhavi, her face ashen, opened her mouth and shut it again.

The king persisted. 'Did you?'

She caught herself this time. 'The anklets are the most beautiful gift that any king has ever given me.

They surpass in beauty and value everything I have ever seen. I shall dance tonight wearing those anklets.'

Neduncheliyan smiled.

The minister intervened. 'Madhavi, I am sorry to bring you here, but can you tell us if this is the Chera prince you met in Vanchi?'

'This man?' Madhavi pointed to Uthiyan. 'This one?'

'Yes. That is the man.'

Madhavi stared at Uthiyan, looking him up and down, staring at him so deeply he felt that she could read his soul.

She was silent.

It was as if time froze. She stared at him.

Her hard, intent expression softened, and it seemed to Uthiyan that her eyes filled with tears.

The minister shifted. 'Is he?'

She looked at the minister and back again at Uthiyan. 'No,' she replied, her voice quavering. 'I do not know this man.'

'Will you excuse me?' She addressed the king. 'May I leave?'

The king nodded and Madhavi walked out of the chambers.

Uthiyan gaped, astounded.

Before he could say anything else, Neduncheliyan mumbled again. 'Get rid of them – these . . . these impostors.' He slumped back on his couch, as if exhausted.

At the king's orders guards surrounded Uthiyan. One of them pushed him, while another roughly grabbed Kannaki's arm. She squealed.

Angry, Uthiyan made to push the guard away, but another one punched him in the face. He fell over, his breath knocked out of him, sinking to his knees.

'Be careful with her,' Uthiyan pleaded. 'Can you not see she is pregnant?'

'You monks are all the same,' the guard sneered, dragging Uthiyan out into the corridor, 'you're in fact the most corrupt still enjoying the pleasures of the flesh while pretending to be holy.'

The amaiccar, waiting in the corridor, was livid. 'How dare you insult me – and that too in front of the king! How dare you!' He spat at Uthiyan. 'You have made a fool out of me.'

He slammed his fist again into Uthiyan's stomach.

Again and again.

36

The pain was unbearable. Uthiyan bent double, nursing his stomach, Kannaki beside him, outside the palace gates. Yet, he could not stop thinking, in spite of the pain. There had to be others who could vouch for him. Paranar, Kapilar – they had been to his father's court in Vanchi. There must have been a Pandya duta who had visited the court of the Cheras.

He could try again. He had to try again.

He turned to Kannaki. 'I've got an idea,' he said to her, 'there are others who can vouch for me. I'm going to try again.'

But Kannaki merely pointed at the sky. Uthiyan looked up. The sun was waning, it was evening. In an hour or so, the sun would descend, and night would wrap and sheathe the city in darkness. Sunset was the hour scheduled for Kovalan's execution.

'There's no time,' Kannaki replied dully.

They made their way to where the execution was to take place, not far from the palace. People had already gathered. Just as Uthiyan pushed his way to the front of the crowd, a covered wagon was brought up to the makeshift platform that had been set up for the execution.

Kannaki clutched Uthiyan's hand tightly as guards brought out a bound Kovalan from the wagon. The executioner led her husband up on to the platform.

She cried out. 'Kovalan!'

Kovalan turned to look at her – and Uthiyan was shocked at his appearance. This was not the indulged, spoilt youth he had met just a day earlier.

In a day, Kovalan had changed. There were bruises where the guards had hit him, a thin line of blood from a cut lip. But it was his expression that struck Uthiyan hard – the haunted, dazed look of a man with no hope.

Kovalan gazed at Kannaki as if there was nothing left in the world.

A pair of guards grabbed his arms, and another held him from behind, pushing him down and holding him in place. The executioner held his sword aloft.

He then swung his sword, and Kovalan jerked

backwards. The blow missed his neck, but cut into his skull. Blood spurted out. Kovalan screamed.

Despite having grown up in a palace, Uthiyan had never before seen an execution.

This was nothing like what he had imagined.

The guards gripped him tighter, and Kovalan was pulled forward again. The executioner swung again, and this time managed to hit Kovalan's neck. A fountain of blood spouted out, spraying the crowd, and Kovalan screamed again.

He was still alive.

The crowd roared. Uthiyan turned away, unable to bear the sight of Kovalan's death.

Instead, he watched the faces around. He was aghast to see excitement, something not too far from pleasure in some, revelling in this bloody, gory execution. Others wept. Yet there were many, to Uthiyan's surprise, bursting with anger, who shook their fists at the guards and the executioner. The king's justice did not seem to be popular with all of his subjects.

The executioner hacked and hacked – it took a number of blows to sever Kovalan's head from his body. Kannaki, unable to bear it, fainted and crumpled to the ground. Uthiyan struggled to pull her up, and discovered that her clothes were wet. Her legs were dripping with water. He dragged her to the edge of the crowd. A group of women standing there helped him lay her down on the ground.

The women clucked, as they noticed her wet clothes. 'She's near her time.'

'What?' Uthiyan was startled. 'She's not due for months!'

'It happens sometimes that the baby comes early,' a woman replied. 'Where do you live? She will need a midwife soon.'

Together, they carried Kannaki down the street. It was impossible. The crowd was large and unruly, and Kannaki, barely conscious, had begun to toss and scream.

Her screams were unbearable.

A palanquin passed by. Uthiyan, with all the air in his lungs, cried out, 'Stop! Help us!'

The palanquin stopped, and a delicate hand parted the curtains.

Uthiyan found himself staring into Madhavi's face for the second time that day.

'Uthiyan!' Sattan was standing by the head of the palanquin. 'What are you doing here?'

Uthiyan stumbled for words, but it was Madhavi who spoke first, looking around at the knot of women kneeling by Kannaki's semiconscious form. 'What is happening?'

One of the women who had been helping Uthiyan replied. 'She's about to birth.'

This was the last person Uthiyan wanted to ask for help, but he had to. He took a deep breath. 'Will you please help us?'

Madhavi signalled her bearers to place the litter down. She alighted from her palanquin. 'Quick,' she told the women, 'lay her there.'

'What about you?'

'I'll manage.' Madhavi replied. 'You'll need a midwife.'

Sattan spoke up. 'I'll help find one. Where do you need to take her?'

Uthiyan told him, and then directed the palanquin bearers. As Sattan darted off, the bearers picked up the litter, and Uthiyan turned to Madhavi. 'Thank you.'

She nodded.

He started to follow the palanquin.

'Wait,' came Madhavi's voice. 'Before you go, what happened?'

'Her husband,' Uthiyan replied, choking back a sob. 'He died because of me. I gave him a dagger, the king thought it was mine – and had him executed for theft and murder. He was tortured, I think, too. But he knew nothing about me or who I was.'

Madhavi gasped. 'I had no idea.'

'How could you?' Uthiyan responded sadly.

'I-I thought I was protecting you.' Madhavi buried her head in her hands, disconsolate. 'I did it for you.'

37

Each cry that Kannaki uttered was like a damnation, an inhuman sound, the cry of a trapped, wounded beast. It was agony, like knife cutting into skin. Sattan, sitting next to him, winced, and paced the room. Uthiyan covered his ears, but even then he could not escape the screaming.

Finally, a spell of silence.

The midwife emerged with Madari. Uthiyan could not help but notice that their hands and garments were bloody.

'She's had a girl,' the midwife told Uthiyan. 'But the child has come too early, and will not last long.'

'And neither will Kannaki,' Madari added. 'She's calling for you.'

Uthiyan rose. Sattan stood up to accompany him, but Uthiyan gestured to him to wait.

With trepidation, Uthiyan entered the room. Kannaki was huddled in a corner, an impossibly small bundle clasped tightly to her. He moved closer, and saw that the baby was asleep, its tiny, red, wrinkled face lying on Kannaki's breast.

Too small to be a real child, Uthiyan thought.

Kannaki turned towards him. Despite her exhaustion, she looked up at him with an expression of wonder. 'So you really are a prince?'

Uthiyan smiled tenderly. 'Do you think so?'

Kannaki sighed and gripped her child tightly. 'Why did the courtesan lie, then?'

Uthiyan shrugged. 'I think she believed she was protecting me.'

'Why?'

Uthiyan struggled for words. 'There was a plot to put me on the throne instead of my brother, and then I was attacked. I didn't want to be king. I wanted to escape that fate. So I went into hiding, hoping that no one would find me. But fate caught up with me. Madhavi knew I didn't want to be king, and I suppose she thought she was helping me escape that.'

Kannaki shook her head. 'The world doesn't make any sense. A prince who doesn't want to be a king –'

'It's a long story–'

'And an innocent man dies! For no reason.' She was weeping now. 'None of this makes any sense.'

Uthiyan felt helpless. 'I didn't mean for any of this to happen. I only wanted to help. But everything good I have tried to do – it has turned rotten, and spawned something terrible.'

'What is your real name?' Kannaki asked.

'Uthiyan.'

'Uthiyan,' she repeated the name, slowly. 'Uthiyan,' she said softly. 'I don't blame you.'

Uthiyan opened his mouth to speak, but shut it again. He didn't know what to say.

'The baby – call her Manimekelai.'

'Kannaki . . .'

She hushed him. 'Don't say anything. I'm tired. Too much has happened.' She shut her eyes and turned her face away.

Uthiyan sat next to her for some time, watching her sleep, the gentle rise and fall of her breath. He thought back to that impossibly brave girl he had met in the forest, who had climbed up a banyan tree to escape a tiger. At first he had thought her simple, ordinary. As he had got to know her, he discovered that the simplicity was but a facade that concealed irrepressible delight, wonder, inexhaustible curiosity. Her endless irritating questions. Her ceaseless thirst for stories. How she had plagued him then!

What he would'nt give to go back to that time, to have a second chance, to do it all over again and hope for a better ending.

The midwife entered, just at that moment. 'How is she?'

'Asleep, I believe.'

The midwife bent over, and touched Kannaki's face. She frowned, and then shook her head. 'No. She's dead.'

She's dead. The words kept playing over and over again, like a mantra, in Uthiyan's mind.

Kannaki was dead.

He could feel the pain rise within him, an itch under his skin, like a demon tightening its hold around his heart, crushing his ribs, suffocating him, a blood-red haze that filled his mind and his body.

He had to get away, he had to get away from this pain that was like an iron hand clamping down his heart, squeezing it so tightly, making it impossible to breathe.

He had to breathe.

He had to get away.

'Uthiyan,' Sattan shouted out, as Uthiyan reached the door, and exited the house. 'Where are you going?'

'I have to go, I have to go now,' Uthiyan stuttered. 'I can't be here.' He stepped out into the night.

Sattan followed him. 'Let me come with you.'

Uthiyan gritted his teeth and shook his head. 'No. Don't follow me!'

'Uthiyan . . .'

'Get away from me!' Uthiyan screamed.

Sattan pleaded. 'Uthiyan, I'm your friend, your best friend.'

'No.' Uthiyan shook his head again, violently. 'You're not. You are sleeping with Madhavi.'

'Uthiyan–'

'You can't deny it! You wanted her then, before, I knew it. I knew it! What kind of friend are you?'

Sattan looked away. 'Forgive me . . .'

'What kind of friend are you?' Uthiyan burst out once more. It felt good to hurt Sattan. Every angry word released some of the pain seething within him.

He kept walking. Sattan called out after him. 'Where are you going?'

'I don't know.'

'Let me come with you.'

'No.' Uthiyan picked up his pace. 'Death follows me.'

Sattan snorted, exasperated. 'You aren't making any sense.'

Uthiyan wheeled about to face him. 'None of this makes sense. Why did any of this happen? What was that prophecy all about? Why did Vel Pekan's wife die? Why did this girl die too?'

'I don't know.'

'You have no answers for me!' Uthiyan shouted. 'What am I supposed to do?

'Come, Uthiyan, come back with me. Come back, please.' Sattan tried again.

'Where to? Where will we go?'

'We'll go somewhere safe, I promise.' Sattan reached out to grasp Uthiyan's hand.

'No. There is nowhere that is safe.' He pushed Sattan away. Sattan stumbled.

'Uthiyan!'

But Uthiyan was running now, despair, anger and grief granting him speed.

'Uthiyan!' Sattan cried out again, gasping, running behind him, but Uthiyan knew that Sattan could not catch up with him.

'Uthiyan! He called out again weakly and Uthiyan looked back. He could not see Sattan any longer.

He ran and ran and ran, through the streets, out of the city and into the darkness that swallowed him whole.

38

For three days, he just lay there. In the middle of the forest that skirted the Vaigai river, waiting for a wild beast, or for hunger or thirst to slay him. The sun passed overhead, followed by the stars, again and again. He heard the calls of forest birds, the lows of predators, the squawks and squeaks and roars that were forest life. A troupe of ants roamed over his body. A squirrel came close to sniff at him cautiously.

And yet death didn't come.

Uthiyan waited and waited.

At the end of the third day, as the sun set, something came. He heard it coming – movements through the tall forest grass, the crunch of fallen leaves, vibrations that spread through the ground beneath him.

He waited.

But it wasn't a tiger or some other beast. It was men.

'Look what we have here!' a voice cried out.

'A spy!' another voice remarked.

A torch was thrust into his face. Uthiyan blinked at the sudden light.

'Not a spy! A monk,' another voice cried out, incredulous.

Uthiyan blinked again, and the torch was withdrawn. He could make out the face of another soldier, grizzled and weatherbeaten, staring at him.

They pulled him up, unresisting. 'Speak!'

Uthiyan was mute. What could he say? Somehow, it just didn't matter. He didn't care what they did. He didn't care who they were. He didn't care about anything any longer.

Nothing mattered.

The soldier slapped him. 'Who are you?'

Uthiyan remained silent.

'What's wrong with him?' the other soldier asked. 'Why doesn't he say anything?'

The first soldier shook his head.

'What do we do with him? '

The soldier cursed. 'We'll have to take him to the commander.'

Uthiyan was half dragged, half led through the forest, to the narrowest ford of the river, and then splashing through water, to the other side, where hidden by a hill of stone, a thick copse of trees and a hastily erected wall – there was an encampment.

Despite the inertia that overwhelmed him, Uthiyan could not ignore the signs of military activity. This was an army camp. But he could tell that this was not his father's army, nor that of the Cholas – nor could it be the Pandya army, now in Korkai.

So whose vast army was this?

It must be the Kalabhras.

Uthiyan was shoved into a tent, brightly lit with torches. A man sat hunched over maps and scrolls, fingers tracing paths on the maps.

'Look what we found, sir!' The soldier, still holding on to Uthiyan, exclaimed.

The man looked up.

And Uthiyan found himself staring at a familiar face.

It was Antuvan. His jaw dropped. 'Oh my Prince, what has happened to you?'

39

Antuvan fed him with his own hands. For three days, Uthiyan hadn't felt a twinge of hunger. Now, suddenly, a ravenous hunger grabbed him. He wolfed down the food.

Antuvan scrutinized him. His expression was unfathomable, hard to read in the flickering light of the one lamp that illuminated his tent. But Antuvan moved closer, and now Uthiyan could tell that there was pity there, and some anger too.

And the story came pouring out of him, in bits and pieces, stammers and stutters. It was like a torrent of words that he couldn't dam, that had lain buried inside him. He told Antuvan all of it – about his mother's plotting, his father's repudiation, the assassination attempt; of his journey with Sattan and Madhavi, of Queen Kannaki's death and the intrigues that followed him to Ay.

And then he told him of the other Kannaki, of Kovalan, and how things had ended so miserably, so terribly in Madurai.

Antuvan listened.

'Prince,' he finally said, after Uthiyan stopped. 'What do you want?'

'I don't know.'

'What do you feel?'

That was easy to answer. 'Anger.' It coursed through him like a raging river, sluicing through every dam, pouring into his body, every drop of blood fermenting into a maddening voice in his mind that demanded justice.

Justice for Kannaki's death. He had to exact justice.

'Justice.' He looked up at Antuvan. 'That's what I want. For Kannaki and Kovalan.'

Antuvan nodded and stood up. 'Sleep now,' he said, gesturing to a pallet laid out in the corner of the tent, 'and we'll talk more in the morning.'

40

The next morning Antuvan showed him around. As they strolled through the camp, Antuvan told him his story. After leaving Vanchi, he had ventured north, to a place where, rumour had it, an army like none other was being assembled.

'An army of faith,' Antuvan said, which bred men as hard as rock. His skills, his knowledge were valued there. They were not men after power, they were men with a vision of a new world, of righteous war – not war fought merely for glory, as the kings of the past had done.

'I am grateful to you,' Antuvan added. 'For without freedom and the anklet you gave me, I would have never found them.'

Uthiyan listened to him silently. It seemed so long ago now, though it had merely been a few months.

'This is the most organized and disciplined force I have ever been part of,' Antuvan told Uthiyan. 'And they are good men too.'

'Trustworthy?' Uthiyan asked with a smile.

Antuvan smiled back. 'Yes,' he replied.

~

Like the camp that Uthiyan saw with Pekan, Antuvan's was clean, almost ruthless in its efficiency and organization. There were no musicians, save for a handful of drummers. No clowns, no dancing girls – Antuvan spat in distaste at the thought.

'We live like monks here.' He smiled, with a glance at Uthiyan's raiment. 'Did you know that our leader was once a monk? You would fit right in with us.'

Uthiyan was intrigued by this story. 'Tell me about him.'

Antuvan stopped walking. 'He is a man of unsurpassed vision. A man of great, intense faith. He has no family, no children, no court – yet he has brought together different kinds of men into one great army, an army I have never seen before.'

He paused. 'He was a soldier once, I believe he was from a noble family, in service to a king whose lands border the Palai lands up north. But something happened, he lost faith in his king, and sought the life of a monk.'

Uthiyan frowned. 'And then what happened? How did he renounce that?'

'I don't think he has completely renounced that path. He was, in time, disillusioned with the ascetic community. He told me that he found the same petty grievances, the same appetites and sins there too – the monks were no better nor worse than the rest of us. And to add to that, he felt they were selfish, believing that their path, one that distanced them from the rest of the world, was a better path. They perceived evil and injustice but did nothing to alleviate them. This did not sit well with our leader. All of the practices he had learnt, the meditative techniques, the mantras, the penances – they could change one person, and bring peace to that person, but they were not being used to eradicate suffering for all. So he chose to return to this world, and to his former occupation of being a soldier, determined to use what he knew, his skills, to end the evil and injustice he perceived.'

He took Uthiyan into a makeshift armoury filled with spears, daggers, swords, shields and all manner of bows and arrows. But there was something even stranger – something that Uthiyan had not seen before – great works of metal, the size of idols. What were these things?

'I had heard tales of these,' Antuvan replied, 'from the time that your ancestor went to war with Athiyaman Neduman Anji of Tagadur. An old man told me about them, he had been a soldier in the army, and he spoke of these great things.' He explained that one was a mechanical bow – it could spit out a series of arrows on its own. Another was a giant sling – when mounted on a battlement, it could fling stones on to forces that tried to climb up the walls. Another, with a giant handle in the shape of a monkey, was a device that, Antuvan claimed, could bite off heads.

Uthiyan marvelled at these contraptions, stroking the monkey head, admiring, with reverence, the many-stringed mechanical bow that spanned the width of a tent.

'And yet these things did not help Athiyaman in his last battle.' Antuvan sighed. 'He seems to have been a man ahead of his time.'

'Perhaps too far ahead.'

As they left the armoury, Uthiyan saw a group of soldiers briskly completing their routines. Moving smoothly, rhythmically, as if in a dance, swooping beneath the sharp, murderous edge of their opponent's sword by just a hair's breadth. Long swords clashing, bronze shields blazing in the sunlight, bodies glistening with the sheen of sweat.

There was, for all his distaste of war, something elegant here – in their precise, fluid movements, in the way these soldiers had trained and perfected the art of killing. Yes, they had made it into an art – war was a dance for these warriors, brutal yet beautiful. Perhaps this is what it was for his father – something noble; an art, just like any other, to perfect and practise.

But this place was not for him. Oh yes, he could shed the robes of a monk and don the vestments of a warrior, and claim his rightful heritage as a scion of two great dynasties. For a moment, Uthiyan desperately wanted to – to feel that sense of belonging that had eluded him, that had been stolen from him the moment the Velir chief's astrologer had made his outrageous prediction.

No, no, no.

It was as if Antuvan had heard his thoughts. 'You should join us, Prince.'

Uthiyan shook his head forcefully. 'No, this life is not for me. I am not a warrior.'

Antuvan glanced around, and then, dragged

Uthiyan to the command tent. He made sure that the flap was fastened securely, before pulling out a scroll of a map.

He stabbed a finger near the outline of a river. 'Here. This is where we are. This is the main part of our army.' He moved his finger eastwards, towards the outline of the coast. 'A smaller force is out there, with our leader, on the plains of Korkai, battling the Komahan. But he sent me here with the larger part of our forces to take Madurai.'

'So Korkai was a ruse to draw out the army?' Uthiyan frowned.

Antuvan nodded. 'But Madurai is merely the beginning for us. Our ruler has his sights on the other kingdoms of Tamilaham, he will not stop at Madurai – and he will need good men, with the ability and knowledge to rule, to govern in his stead.'

He clapped a hand on Uthiyan's shoulder. 'Join us, Prince, I know our leader would welcome the kind of man you are – a prince of royal blood, but whose heart beats for the common people – with open arms. You could help us a great deal. You were born to rule. You could rule here in Madurai when we take it.'

'No.'

'Our leader heard that you might be in Aykudi. He sent emissaries to meet you there, to make an alliance with you. I know he would want this.' Antuvan smiled. 'Think of it, Prince. I heard of the prophecy that was cast – the same prophecy that caused you and I to meet, and the events that it set in motion have brought us to meet a second time. You are trying to escape your fate, Prince. Perhaps destiny does demand that you rule. Perhaps it has created these circumstances – the horrific miscarriage of justice that you witnessed – to prod you, to awaken you to what you must do. Perhaps it speaks again, here, in my voice, to you, providing you with another chance, another opportunity. You cannot deny who you are, what you are. This is your fate. It will pursue you.'

Uthiyan could not help but wonder at Antuvan's words. His resolve trembled. Perhaps he was wrong. Perhaps Antuvan was right.

'I am right,' Antuvan said, seeming to decipher his thoughts again. 'That prophecy might have meant that you are destined to be a king. Perhaps not the king of the Cheras. But the king of Madurai. And as such a king, history will ensure that you outshine your brother. Doesn't it make sense?'

Uthiyan was silent.

Antuvan persisted. 'Doesn't it?'

'It could,' Uthiyan had to agree.

'We march tonight,' Antuvan told him. 'In the

darkness, so that we reach Madurai by first light. We have informants inside the city who have already been instructed to poison the moat, so that the city is cut off from fresh water, and so that the crocodiles in the moat are killed – making our job easier. But before we leave, if you agree, I want you to speak to our soldiers. I want you to tell them of what you have seen in Madurai, so that they know, they are assured, that they fight for the right side, the right cause. We fight not to steal, not merely for glory, but also for justice. And that is the kind of kingdom you are destined to rule.'

He stepped out of the tent. Uthiyan was left alone, staring at the map before him. He thought back to when Paranar spoke of the Kalabhras for the first time. He had spoken of harsh, unyielding men, bred of stone – and now Uthiyan had met them. A new age, Paranar had said, was dawning.

Perhaps Antuvan was right. Perhaps his destiny had found him.

He stepped out of the tent and joined Antuvan. 'Perhaps you are right.'

'I am right.' Antuvan's harsh, scarred face broke into a smile. He pulled his own weapon out – a nicked, gleaming sword, and handed it to Uthiyan. 'This is yours now.'

Uthiyan inhaled. He knew how to use a sword, but he had never killed a man. Is this what his destiny demanded of him?

~

At first light, Uthiyan found himself exhausted after a night of marching through the dark forest. The sword by his side was heavy, it felt like a burden. They were within sight of Madurai's walls.

Already, the Pandyan forces guarding Madurai had news of the Kalabhras march, and they were gathered there on the field to meet them.

But the Pandyan forces were pitifully small, a garrison merely to man the city while the bulk of the army was in Korkai defending the fisheries.

It would be a rout, an easy win for the Kalabhras. Uthiyan could already see that.

'Uthiyan!' Antuvan signalled Uthiyan to join him at the head of the army.

As Uthiyan made his way to Antuvan, he heard him cry out, 'We have a Chera prince, one born to rule, in our midst! Destiny has foretold that he will be a great king, one whose fame will eclipse his peers. He renounced his birthright, and he has come here, to join us, to help us defeat the Pandyas and take their throne. He has come to join us. The Kalabhras army!'

Antuvan raised his sword, and the soldiers cheered.

The noise was deafening. Uthiyan took his place beside Antuvan, who clapped one hand on his shoulder.

'Here he is. I met him for the first time in a prison in Vanchi. I was condemned to die. But this prince believed that I was a good man, that I deserved to live, and so he set me free.'

This elicited another loud cheer.

'He saved my life – but it cost him the throne.'

No, it did not, Uthiyan thought – he was getting it all wrong. Before he could stop him or say something, Antuvan went on.

'And it brought him to Madurai, where he witnessed something horrific, something that we seek to put right today, in this battle, in this fight. And today we will give him another throne, in exchange for the one he lost.' Antuvan turned to Uthiyan. 'Tell them what you saw, Prince.'

Uthiyan took a deep breath, staring at the thousands of faces before him. Grizzled faces, faces of youths, faces of veterans, faces that had been maimed in war before. They were waiting for him to speak. He felt tension knot in his belly. They were waiting for *him*, waiting to listen to *him*.

The excitement. The thrill. He had never felt anything like it before. Surging through the hordes of soldiers, moving through him, binding them together. It was something powerful. Divine, even.

He opened his mouth – and somehow, miraculously, the words spilled out of him. The right words. It was the story of Kannaki and Kovalan that he told them – of the charming, insouciant, pregnant girl he met in a forest, and how he came with her to Madurai, to help her meet her love, her husband.

He told them then of the king's justice, how Kovalan was wrongly accused of a crime he didn't commit, how he was wrongly condemned to death, how he and Kannaki struggled for justice, but they were not believed, and an innocent man was executed.

He told them of the king, Neduncheliyan, of the scandals that rocked his court, of how they distracted him from his duty to rule and govern.

He told them of Kannaki's death in childbirth, brought about by the distress of watching her husband die. He told them of his own pain, of his desire for revenge, for justice.

For Kannaki.

The soldiers screamed. War cries filled the air. Uthiyan was stunned. Dizzy. It was headier than any liquor he had ever tasted. Better than sex. Greater than any pleasure he had known before.

This wave that swelled through him, through all those before him, it was magic. It was powerful.

Antuvan pulled him into a rough embrace and then thrust one hand towards the city walls, and the Pandya forces amassed before them.

The army roared. And then, like a mighty river breaking a dam, they burst on to the plains of Madurai.

Book 4

Madurai

41

It was over so fast.

All Uthiyan could remember afterwards was the sight of arrows raining from the sky. The clang of swords, the slick, wet, sick sound of steel sliding into flesh. War cries. The whirl of steel, flashing in the noonday sun, dazzling arcs cutting through the air, bone and flesh. Blood spurting like a fountain of rubies. The beat of war drums, punctuated by blood-curdling shrieks.

And then, a strange moment of silence. A river of blood flowed on the parched earth of the fields outside Madurai.

The caw of a bird. Uthiyan looked up, and already he could sight vultures and birds of carrion wheeling overhead, waiting.

He looked at the sword in his hand. He hadn't even used it. The blade was clean. No blood on it.

What was this? What was he doing here?

But there was no time to think. Antuvan flashed past, on a horse, his sword aloft. 'Men!' he shouted. 'Onwards. To the wall.'

Uthiyan looked to the wall. The moat skirting it was half empty. There, the corpse of a crocodile was already being attacked by a vulture. Even as he watched, one of the Kalabhras companies, with siege ladders mounted atop an elephant, waded through the sludge of the moat.

The ground before him, the path that led to the wall, was littered with the dead and dying. Men screaming in agony, clutching their wounds. The reek of blood, flesh, sweat and faeces. Ruptured guts, entrails spilling on to the earth. Dead bodies, still spasming. The headless trunk of a soldier writhing on the battlefield. Closer by, a severed hand, fingers still convulsing.

A young boy, lying on the ground, not far from Uthiyan, cried out. Bloodstained fingers clutched a flesh wound, a cut in his stomach that was too wide, too big for any needle. 'Help,' he pleaded, unable to bear the pain. 'Help me, please.'

Uthiyan stared at him, not knowing what to do, a fist pressed to his mouth to stop himself from vomiting.

'Have you no stomach for this?' A Kalabhras soldier behind Uthiyan pushed him out of the way. Kneeling, he pressed a hand to the boy's forehead, and then with a quick stroke of his dagger, slashed the boy's throat. Blood dripped on to the ground, as the boy's eyes rolled back, and his body turned limp.

Uthiyan turned to the side, and retched.

The soldier watched him. The ground seemed to lurch beneath Uthiyan's feet, the battlefield swimming before him. He was falling . . . he could not pull himself up.

'Come, Prince.' The soldier yanked Uthiyan by the scruff of his neck and pulled him through the field.

The soles of Uthiyan's feet slid on bloodstained, upturned earth. Over stones and broken-off arrowheads. Over squishy things that felt like flesh. Over blood and bone. He shut his eyes.

42

The city on the other side of the wall was on fire. The Kalabhras troops sped towards the palace, but Uthiyan, watching the red-gold flames spreading, thought of Madari and Kannaki's baby. The deafening sound of drums filled the air – the large drum in the palace was being sounded to alert all that an attack was under way.

He hesitated for a moment, watching the troops winding their way through smoke-filled streets, towards the palace.

He was meant to accompany them to the palace.

He could not desert them.

He was to be their ruler after all.

And yet he found himself turning the other way, to the streets that led to Madari's house.

The fire hadn't spread to this quarter as yet, but all the houses were bolted. The street was eerily quiet. He stopped in front of Madari's house.

'Madari!' he shouted. 'It's Uthiyan.'

The door opened a chink. He caught a glimpse of Madari's worried, pinched face.

'What is happening?'

'It's the Kalabhras. They've come into the city. Some of the houses are on fire. You better go.'

She sighed heavily. 'But where can I go?'

'Somewhere safe.'

She shook her head sadly. 'There is nowhere that is safe. I will stay here.'

Uthiyan cursed inwardly. She was right. He pulled himself together. 'What happened to the child?'

'Your friend took her. He came last night, as soon as they heard of the Kalabhras army on the move. He was going to Puhar, perhaps he will take the child to Kovalan's parents.'

'Why didn't you go with them? You could have at least got out of the city.'

Madari shrugged. 'Where is there to go to for an old woman like me?

As she spoke, Uthiyan became aware that the drums had stopped. Surprised, he paused.

Madari too looked stunned. She turned to Uthiyan. 'They must have breached the palace. That's why the drums have stopped.'

~

The streets were seething – knots of men fighting, houses and shops being broken into and looted. The fire was spreading fast, smoke rising to squat above the city, dark and ominous.

Uthiyan found himself stopping by a jeweller's shop. The jeweller, laden with golden necklaces and clothed in the most expensive orange silk, cowered on the floor of his shop, while a youth stood over him, a rusty sword gripped tightly in one hand

'Don't do this,' the jeweller begged. 'Just take everything and go.'

'You dismissed me unjustly, without wages,' the youth spat out. 'This is the time for revenge and justice – that's what the Kalabhras are saying. I will take everything and go, your life too!' He plunged the sword into the jeweller.

Uthiyan gasped. The jeweller was bleeding to death, as the youth, grabbing a fistful of loose gems, stepped over his body and out of the shop.

'Go,' the jeweller, croaked to Uthiyan, as he pressed

his hands against the wound, trying to staunch the blood. 'You can't do anything for me. At least I don't have to live to watch Madurai crumble and fall.'

'Don't say that!'

'You are young,' the jeweller wheezed. 'And the young are full of hope.'

'The Kalabhras will be better than the Pandyas.'

The jeweller, now pale with the loss of blood and close to death, shook his head.

43

The palace thronged with people. Not just Kalabhras soldiers, but an assortment of townspeople ripping semi-precious gems out of the pillars, hacking away at the gold and silver pendants that hung down from the roof, ripping out pearl-encrusted canopies.

In the corridors Uthiyan was shocked to find bodies – of palace servants, guards, courtiers, handmaidens – sprawled, earrings ripped from ear lobes, fingers hacked off for their rings.

Uthiyan followed the trail of bodies to the inner courtyard, where, in a cordoned area, the ancient tree sacred to the Pandyas, the kadamba tree, was being cut down. Antuvan stood before it, supervising its destruction.

'Prince Uthiyan!' he exclaimed. 'Come here.'

Uthiyan ventured closer and stopped, stunned. In front of Antuvan, a body lay spreadeagled by the roots of the tree. It was Neduncheliyan, the king.

Uthiyan stared in horror. For Neduncheliyan's eyes were bulging, his mouth gaping open in a silent scream, as if he was staring into the face of Death itself. There was a red slash on his throat, tendons and muscles exposed, blood dripping down a heavy necklace of gold, emeralds and corals, past his brocaded silk garments, congealing at the base of the tree.

'How did he die?' He could not help asking.

'We found him dead,' Antuvan replied, and gestured to a bloodstained dagger lying nearby. 'He killed himself by his own hand.'

But Uthiyan, staring at the horrified expression on the king's face wondered otherwise – if this was truly the face of a man who had chosen his own death.

Somehow . . . he couldn't quite believe it.

The sound of furious banging on a door, followed by a series of wails, made him start. Uthiyan looked up, startled. Antuvan gestured to a door in the adjacent corridor, locked and guarded by a fierce-looking soldier. 'We've locked the womenfolk and the Perumdevi in there.'

'Why?'

'To prevent them from getting away, of course. The Komahan in not here, he is at Korkai with most of the army. We might need hostages.'

What fate would befall these women? Uthiyan was overcome with rage. 'This is wrong.' He gestured to the sprawling corpse of a palace courtier, not far from his king. 'This too.'

'No change is bloodless,' Antuvan replied tersely. 'The price is often paid in blood. But it is worth it.'

He bent down, and before Uthiyan's eyes, pulled off the king's bejewelled necklace.

44

Uthiyan wandered, as if in a dream, through scenes of desecration. Each room told a similar story. Bloodstains on the floor, figures lying face down, claimed by death. Soldiers and commoners alike, scurrying quickly down corridors, gems and priceless objects clutched tightly in their hands.

Uthiyan's heart sank. War, no matter what the cause, the pretext, seemed to always look the same – the same story each time. How often had his father done this?

Had his brother done this?

Outside the palace, the silver pattimandapam, the source of so much of Neduncheliyan's glory and greatness, was on fire. The silver walls were alight with the red-gold flames. A crowd had gathered – and to Uthiyan's surprise, they cheered.

As he watched, a soldier ran past him, his arms full of scrolls, towards the fire.

'Wait!' Uthiyan called out. 'What are you doing with those?'

The soldier paused for an instant. 'Burning them.'

Uthiyan gasped. 'You can't!'

The soldier responded with a leery grin. 'Commander's orders. We're burning all of these.'

As he spoke he edged towards the fire, and Uthiyan, following him, was appalled to see pile upon pile of scrolls and palm-leaf manuscripts withering to ashes in the flames.

The crowd cheered again as the soldier tossed his bundle of scrolls into the fire.

'Why are you doing this?' Uthiyan shouted, appalled. 'These are priceless.'

The soldier examined a scroll closely. 'Just a bunch of words.'

'These are famous poems–'

'The king spent so much on poems and poetry! But nothing on his own people,' a voice called out from the crowd.

Uthiyan whirled around.

'That's right,' another man exclaimed. 'We saw the gifts he gave poets who sang well of him – golden flowers, and food, and expensive garments. Elephants even. And for what? For poems that praised him.'

'No, it was more than that!' Uthiyan whipped around to stare up at the pattimandapam. 'This was the seat of the Sangam. This–'

But the crowd had no patience for Uthiyan. 'All those poets lived off the king,' another voice piped in, angrily. 'Those poems were not for us. And now all of those poets have fled. Why do you want to preserve that? Those are just empty verses!'

Uthiyan stared in anguish at the fire spreading up the building, winding like a creeper along the length, up and down the pillars, chasing down the seats where the forty-nine had sat, across the scrolls and manuscripts of the best works that poets had produced for centuries. Exquisite poems, manuals of dance and art and poetry, histories and treatises.

All of it turning to ash. All of it, the beauty, the glory, the pain, the love of the past. The house of the Sangam that he heard of for years, whose tales had filled his dreams. Whose poems travelled up and down the length of Tamilaham, entertaining both courts and villages alike.

How could he explain it to these people – what they stood to lose in the anger of a moment?

This was terrible.

He lurched towards the fire, picking up a tattered palm leaf here, another there, struggling to preserve what he could.

'Stop him!' he heard a voice cry out from behind him. He ignored it.

A soldier pulled him back roughly from the fire.

Uthiyan turned to him, desperate, cradling the few leaves he had managed to rescue in his arms. 'Help me!'

'Who are you to tell me what to do?' the soldier retorted.

Uthiyan had had enough. The bloodshed, the looting, the pointless deaths – and now this. He pulled himself to his full height, and in his most imperious manner, shot back. 'I am your king!'

The soldier snorted.

Uthiyan was incensed. 'You heard your commander on the battlefield.'

'I heard him and I heard you as well. And then later, on the battlefield, I saw that you didn't even lift your sword.'

'That's right,' another voice exclaimed. Uthiyan turned to see another soldier, a belligerent gleam in his eye, advance towards him. 'That's not the kind of king I want to fight for or live under. Who are you, princeling, to tell us what to do when you cannot even wield a sword?'

Blazing with fury, Uthiyan replied. 'You are an idiot.' He turned to face the crowd, teeth gritted in anger. 'You are all idiots!' he shouted.

'Heard that?'

'He called us idiots!'

'Who does he think he is?'

The crowd broke then, in unison, charging towards Uthiyan. The soldier was the one who got there first. 'You had it coming,' he said, as he punched Uthiyan in the gut.

Blows rained on Uthiyan. He fell to the ground. 'Stop this!'

But the blows came. And Uthiyan found his hand closing into a fist, and punching upwards. His hand connected with something soft. He twisted, and heard a shriek of pain.

And as he heard the scream, something stirred in his mind. A fragment of a memory. A scream like that one, a dark night, in a place thick with trees.

The white glimmer in the trees. The glinting edge of a knife.

Panic racing through him then, as it was racing through him now.

The memory of a man, shaking in fear. The wide, wide whites of his eyes.

The taste of his blood. The sound of a pig being gutted. The gurgle of blood. The look of death on his face.

It was then, as the crowd grew around him, kicking, screaming, tearing at his clothes and at his hair, that Uthiyan remembered.

Remembered that night of the attempt on his life in Vanchi. How three men had cornered him, how something had risen in him, and then – that night – something had possessed him, like a demon or a spirit, riding his skin, and fighting to save his life.

Biting, kicking, screaming, knifing.

He remembered it all.

What had he done?

The blows continued to rain on him. Uthiyan did not resist. He surrendered. He accepted the pain. This was what he deserved, he thought, as agony ripped up his spine, as pain clenched his gut. This was it. This was his destiny. This was why death followed him, seeking his life in return for the lives he had taken.

This was the price he had to pay for the mistakes he had made, over and over again.

This was atonement.

Book 5

Destiny

45

She was standing there before him again, the demoness he knew as Death, the woman he had seen in his dreams and nightmares. Darker than night.

Was this a dream?

Or was this Death?

'Oh no,' the shadow said. 'You have it all wrong, I am not a demoness. I am a goddess.'

'No,' Uthiyan gritted his teeth and spat out. 'You are not. If you were, why have you done this to me?'

'What have I done?' She transformed, and in a moment she was Madhavi, opening her hands in a gesture of entreaty, pleading before him. 'What have I done?'

'You have taken everything away from me. You have killed, and you have made me kill.'

'Nonsense.' She was brusque now. 'I have only taken away your illusions.'

He sank to his knees, broken. 'You have taken away everything and everyone I have loved. You have destroyed it all. You have left me with nothing.' He was weeping now. 'Why have you done this to me?'

She transformed again, and now she was regal, a hint of sorrow in her eyes. She was Kannaki, Pekan's wife, sitting on a swing above the palace gardens. 'Only because I love you.'

'You don't love me,' Uthiyan shook his head, shocked to find himself sounding like Pekan, bitter and angry. 'Your love is a noose around my neck.'

She changed again, and now she was Kovalan, dying, the light fading from his eyes. 'Your love is a noose around my neck,' he repeated. 'You killed me with your love. You killed me with your care.'

'Stop it!' Uthiyan shouted. 'Stop it and let me out of here!'

Kovalan's corpse rose and turned into an insouciant, charming girl, pregnant, laughing, a hand on her rotund belly. 'Tell me a story,' Kannaki simpered. 'You promised! Tell me a story. Not about kings and queens. About common people.'

Uthiyan buried his head in his hands, weeping.

'Sing me a poem,' another voice spoke up. Uthiyan

looked up, and it was Queen Kannaki standing before him. 'Poems move men and kings. Remember that.'

'Then why did Madurai burn?' Uthiyan screamed. 'All that poetry – it was lies! There's no truth in it about what war is like. There's no greatness in it.' He slumped to the floor, defeated.

'Dharma comes to kings in the shape of death,' the queen replied.

And then Antuvan stood before him. 'No change is bloodless.'

'Then kill me too,' Uthiyan spluttered, 'take my life instead of chasing me, and killing those around me. I am not a king but I am a prince, so then kill me too!'

'No.' Death was back before him. 'No.'

'Why not?' Uthiyan was belligerent. 'You have taken everything else! Take me too.'

'No.' Death shook her head again. 'I have left you with a great gift. The thing you desire above all else.'

'You lie.'

Death laughed. 'I have given you my song. You must sing it now. That is your fate.'

46

He struggled to get up. Pain raced through his joints. He screamed, as the surface he was on lurched.

'It's a bad road.' A woman spoke.

Uthiyan gasped in agony. 'Where am I?' He could see nothing.

'You're in a cart, on a bad road. Lie back. Drink this.'

She poured something into his mouth.

Numbness overtook him.

When he awoke, he was told that he was in a community of ascetics, high up in caves in the Samanar hills. His body had been broken and burned. His face and eyes had been injured – he might never see clearly again. The burns would heal, but he would be disfigured for life.

But he would live.

Yet this troubled Uthiyan not. The pain he did not mind. It was other things.

Shame. Anger.

What had he done?

It would have been better if he hadn't lived. If he had died instead.

He remembered that a woman had saved him.

Why had she bothered? He cursed her. It would have been better if she had left him to die.

Not long after, the monks found him, a sharp-edged stone in his hand, a pool of dark blood spreading around him, across the stone floor of his cave.

The ascetics were frightened he would try to kill himself again. They wouldn't leave him alone.

Why am I still alive? Uthiyan asked himself this question every day.

Why had he been spared?

He awoke to a woman's voice. The same woman with the gravelly voice who had brought him here.

'You're awake,' she said.

'Yes.' Bitter silence followed. She had saved his life, but Uthiyan could not find it in himself to be grateful.

She sighed. 'Have you been out?'

Uthiyan shook his head.

'Why not?'

'What's the point?' he growled. 'I can't see.'

'No, but you can feel,' the woman retorted brusquely. 'And believe me, sunlight feels completely different from a dark cave.'

'I can't go out.'

She was persistent. 'I'll help you.'

He was out of the cave, and yes, she was right. Sunlight did feel different. There was a lightness and warmth in the texture of the air. Her touch on his arm guided him.

'How did you bring me here?' he asked.

'I found you outside Madurai, I brought you here. We have met before.'

'Where?' Uthiyan was surprised.

'In Aykudi,' she replied. 'My name is Kavunthy. You were singing a poem that startled a peacock, preening for its mate, and I yelled at you. I was on my way to meet Vel Pekan's wife, Queen Kannaki. We spoke at court too. I warned you not to meddle with Pekan or the Kalabhras. You did not listen to my advice.'

Uthiyan sat down heavily, bursting with grief at the thought of everything that had happened.

'Are you all right?'

'I cannot . . .' he began, struggling to hold the tears back, teeth clenched. 'I cannot . . . I hate you!'

And then he could hold back no longer, and began to sob.

She sat beside him.

'I don't know what to do. I don't know what I have done. I don't know how to go on.'

'What have you done?'

He covered his face. 'Everything. Everything is my fault.'

'You give yourself too much importance.' Kavunthy replied. 'You think you are so important. You think you are the centre of the universe, responsible for everything. The wheel at the centre of everything. No. There are other wheels, and you are just one among many wheels.'

She touched the bandages on his arms. 'The worst is that you do yourself harm in this. This is not ahimsa, this is not the code that we must live by. The worst form of violence is the one that you do to yourself. This means you do not accept yourself.'

'I am a sinner!' Uthiyan shouted. 'I have killed men. How can I live with that?'

'We are all sinners. There is one piece of advice I can give you. We believe we live in a cruel, wretched world, and that moves us to cruel, wretched acts. The world is beautiful. The truth is that the darkness lies within us. You cannot force out darkness, you cannot cut it out or carve it out. How can you cut your own shadow from under your feet? It is impossible. Each one of us must learn to accept the darkness within us, those things we consider too horrible to reveal. And yet, once we learn this, we discover that this same darkness abides in every other soul, hidden away and in secret – and this moves us to an even greater realization – we find our own selves reflected in everyone we meet, we find our own soul in them.'

Uthiyan digested this. 'No.' He shook his head. 'Then you could justify anything on this earth. Any crime, any injustice can be excused. I cannot hold with that.'

'No, you cannot justify a crime or a criminal act. But it is not for us to stand in judgement – we forgive others by forgiving ourselves. We are all sinners, all equally guilty, we are all little wheels. No one is singularly responsible, and yet everybody is responsible. Think back on the cause of your acts, the ones you feel guilty for – were you not pushed to act?'

'Yes, but–'

'So who is responsible for forcing your hand?'

'But then it goes on forever!'

'Which is why forgiveness – and you can start by forgiving yourself – is important. If you do not forgive yourself, you will destroy yourself. And then who is responsible for that?'

'I would be.'

'No,' she replied. 'You would blame me. You would die cursing me, believing that I should have left you to die – and that you must repair that by destroying yourself. Isn't that what you think?' She paused. 'Do you blame yourself for Pekan's wife's death?'

Uthiyan nodded.

'But you could blame me too. I was there. She sent for me to hear her grief. And yet I couldn't save her. Do you place her death too at my feet?'

Uthiyan was silent.

'The truth is that she killed herself,' Kavunthy replied. 'The other things you blame yourself for – they are not entirely of your making. You are not fully responsible, you can never truly be, there are a thousand factors that conspire to produce one event. How can you take on the burden of all of them?'

Uthiyan digested this. 'But how do I forgive myself?'

The nun chuckled. 'The answer is simple, but the action difficult. Think on what has happened to you. Everything. All the discomfort, all the things you'd rather not admit, all the things you would like to hide about yourself. All the sorrow you'd rather not feel. And then think of a way to use those feelings to guide you to do good.

47

The same dream. The nightmare returned that night to Uthiyan. He was not a monk asleep on the rough floor of a cave, but a prince on a silken mattress, tossing and turning, awaiting an assignation with the most beautiful courtesan in Tamilaham.

How different he was now!

He thought about what Kavunthy had said to him. What had been the purpose of all that had happened to him? Of those events that had pushed him out of Vanchi, forcing him to give up his throne, and then that whole awful mess in Aykudi – and then worse in Madurai?

Had he been escaping his destiny – the fact that he was meant to be a king?

But he hadn't been. The prophecy had merely been

a ruse to propel him along his path. To question what it meant to be a king.

The next day, unbidden, a fragment of a song came to Uthiyan. A story that continued to weave itself throughout the day, and the next day, and the day after that. A song that never seemed to end.

It was a story that seemed to tell itself through him. It was not merely his story, although it made use of his experiences, but it was also Madhavi's story, Kannaki's story, Kovalan's story, Kavunthy's story.

He could not shake the image of poems burning, in Neduncheliyan's pattimandapam. Poems that spoke of love, poems that enabled men and women to see the world around them anew.

But poems that also moved men and women to war and violence, that, as the angry crowd that had gathered to burn poems told him, were written to praise and flatter kings, poems that helped pave the way for conquest, poems that dispossessed.

Each day, the song wove itself within him, through him. Everything that was in him – all his grief, rage, love and regret – these shaped the song that he wove.

And then one day, when the story seemed to be close to ending, and his eyesight was good enough to allow him to travel, he left his cave to sing this song.

Epilogue

The Kalabhras had taken Madurai, and now they were to besiege Puhar, making inroads into Chola lands, so Uthiyan heard on his travels. He now had a yal, and with a begging bowl, clad in the clothes of a monk, he travelled from village to town, singing his song. From the smattering of gossip and news he picked up he learnt that the Cheras had escaped the attentions of the Kalabhras, and Shenguttuvan had won renown as a great general on the battlefield.

Tamilaham had not changed in the way that he, Paranar and Vel Pekan had thought – or at least not so fast. Change was coming, but it would take generations for things to shift completely.

Uthiyan was wiser now, older now, and he had learnt that there were always positive and negative aspects to every season of change. His job was to sing the song that had taken hold of him, that seemed to evolve with each retelling. Wherever he went, he seemed to meet a character from his story. Every village, every town had a Madhavi, a Kovalan, a Kannaki, a Neduncheliyan.

And so the poem seemed to shift and grow richer with each telling. It began as a story of thwarted love and inescapable grief, of men and women. It had then grown into a bigger story, a tale also of the rights of common folk and the responsibilities of kings. The burning of the Sangam, too, had taught him that poems were not merely for the amusement of kings. What Kannaki, the queen, had told him so long ago stayed with him – that his words had to have purpose, for they carried power. He must choose his words and their purpose wisely. Change was coming, and it was necessary – necessary for power to be rebalanced, for the rule of kings to be just, for them to listen to those whom they ruled. To be in accord with dharma.

Years went by.

~

Uthiyan was in a village that day, a village that to his ears seemed to be filled with screaming children.

'What's happening?' He asked a child who rushed past him in excitement.

'Adigal, an elephant! An elephant is coming!'

Uthiyan, curious, moved out of the shade of the tree near the village shrine, under which he sat while the afternoon sun heated the air, waiting for dusk to fall, when the village would gather to listen to the next instalment of his evolving epic. He had fasted all day, allowing only water to touch his lips, and had already begun to feel exhausted.

A boy climbed up the tree to get a better look at the elephant. Uthiyan cupped his hands and shouted up, 'Can you see the banner on the elephant?'

'A bow,' the child replied. 'Wait, it's a bow and arrow.'

The insignia of the Cheras.

Uthiyan stiffened. Then, he told himself to relax. They were just passing through. What would a Chera envoy want in this village?

But the procession stopped in the centre of the village, and the village headman rushed out to meet it.

'What's happening now?' Uthiyan asked the boy on the tree.

'He's talking . . .' and then, voice rising with excitement, 'he's coming here!'

The children, buzzing with curiosity, surrounded Uthiyan.

The man approached, close enough for Uthiyan

to get an impression of rich silk, and court manners. He introduced himself as Sanjayan, an envoy of the Chera king.

'Adigal,' he said, as the children tittered, 'the Ko has commanded me to bring you to him.'

The children, racing in circles around Uthiyan, screamed, 'The king!'

Uthiyan was painfully aware that now the village had gathered around him.

Uthiyan looked around, he could barely make out the features of the faces around him, but he could imagine what their expressions on their faces would reveal. Surprise. Excitement. Anticipation.

All Uthiyan felt was dread. The thought of the glittering court. It had once been his life. But what was the point of running, after all these years? The past seemed to have finally caught up with him. It always did. Now his brother had found him. So many years had passed. What kind of king had Shenguttuvan become?

He nodded to Sanjayan, and he picked up his staff and begging bowl, and made his way to the elephant.

'How did you find me?'

The king was on his way back from an expedition, Sanjayan replied, as he helped Uthiyan on to the elephant waiting for them. 'A few days ago, while he was passing through, a village petitioned the king about the misbehaviour of a soldier, and demanded justice.'

He paused, as the elephant began making its way to the Chera camp. 'The king was surprised by their appeal – he listened to them, and justice was done. But rarely do people of this sort have the boldness to approach the king and risk his rage for what was, to the court, a trifling matter. And so the king made deeper enquiries. Then they told him of a monk who had come to them recently and sung to them a poem about how kings too must pay the price for the injustice done to common folk.'

Uthiyan could feel Sanjayan's sharp gaze scrutinize him. 'And then?'

'The king asked for more of this poem, and they told him the story of Madhavi and Kannaki, and the Ko felt, he believed, that it could only have been composed by you. For we knew you had accompanied Madhavi, that you had gone to the court of Vel Pekan. But after that we did not know what had happened to you. The similarities between your journey and this story – they were too striking to ignore. And so the king sent me, his chief of orrar, from village to village, tracing your footsteps, to find you. Each village

I visited told me the same story. And so I found you, by following your poem.'

The envoy lapsed into silence, and Uthiyan was too troubled by his own thoughts to ask any more questions.

Did Shenguttuvan feel abandoned? The years had passed by – who would they be now to each other? Uthiyan wondered.

He gazed at his hands, worn and callused. The soles of his feet were cracked, and he was thin and gaunt, the effect of the strict regimen of fasting he kept. His face was scarred, and his skin beaten by the sun and weather. So different from the youthful, handsome figure he once cut at court.

He wondered at how the courtiers would see him now. They'd mock his shaven head, and the holes in his robes. He could have lived a different life, been a prince – even a king: would they taunt him for being a runaway? A man who sought to escape his destiny, a man who hadn't been brave enough to claim the prize that was the throne? At least, that's how they'd see it. In Vanchi, was he known as a coward?

They had almost reached the king's encampment. Even though Uthiyan's eyesight was blurred, he could see something of the camp, spread out before them, gaining definition as they neared. It was a large affair, spreading out across an entire plain. There was a section for dancing girls, another for trumpeters and musicians. The envoy told him that the king was on his way back from the Himalayas, from a great expedition.

'He carved the Chera crest into a mountain!' Sanjayan exclaimed triumphantly.

Uthiyan had to bite his tongue from asking whether they had managed to spot the Chola tiger there, but this would not do for the dour Sanjayan. What would his brother make of this joke? Was he a stern king, or did he still possess a sense of humour?

And what did his brother want now? A sensation, a prickle of dread, crept down Uthiyan's spine. Could it be possible that Shenguttuvan still thought Uthiyan was a threat to him? What would the years have turned him into? Was he also a fierce, aloof warrior like their father, pragmatic to the point of cruelty?

It was possible that his poem had offended the king – speaking of death and destruction coming to unjust kings. Would his brother see that as criticism? Would the king ask him to take his words back? Perhaps he would execute him as their father might have – no, Uthiyan corrected himself – certainly would have.

~

They had arrived at the king's tent, emblazoned with the Chera insignia. Uthiyan's heart began to beat faster and his stomach knotted in tension. He paused before the entrance, panic seizing him, too afraid to step inside. For years he had thought of his brother, worrying if Shenguttuvan still felt angry at him. How would Shenguttuvan react? Would he be angry or loving? Resentful or forgiving? Would his brother be glad to see him? Or would he curse him?

Sanjayan, gently, nudged him forward. Inside, Uthiyan spotted the flash of swords, of Yavana armour, the silk clothes of courtiers – all of which seemed to belong to another lifetime. The nobles haughty, faces pinched with pride – had he been like that? Uthiyan cringed at the thought.

And on the dais, he glimpsed a woman seated on the throne. Shenguttuvan's queen. He couldn't see clearly but he could make out that she was not beautiful like his mother, Nalchonai. But she was elegant, and there was more of an aura of power to her than his mother had ever had. Her face was familiar. Was it – could it be Ilango Venmal? Uthiyan squinted, and cursed his failing eyesight. Had Shenguttuvan, after all, managed to marry the Velir princess with whom he had been besotted?

It appeared that he had. Uthiyan felt his heart leap

at the thought. And his eyes moved past her, to the man on the throne beside her. His brother.

It had been so long. Uthiyan felt his breath stop, felt tears prickle his eyes.

He could barely make him out, but there was a sense of him, his dark, powerful, brawny presence. For a moment, Uthiyan felt he was in the presence of his father. His brother, as he had aged, seemed more and more like the king, their father. Stiff, commanding, distant on his golden throne.

And then his face broken into a smile.

And to the gasp of the courtiers, the king leapt off the dais. Before Uthiyan could register what was happening he found himself crushed into an embrace. The king was close enough for Uthiyan to see. It was the same brother, just older, weary looking, face burnt by the sun, hair peppered with grey, crow's feet at the corners of his eyes.

How the years had changed them both!

Uthiyan's surprise must have shown, for the king stepped away.

'Brother?' The king was now frowning. 'It is you, isn't it?'

Uthiyan nodded, unable to speak.

The king's eyes searched him. 'Forgive me, it has

been years. I – I thought that you would be happy to see me, but perhaps . . .'

'No,' Uthiyan broke out. 'No . . .'

His vision swam, it was all so much. He felt weak, as if he was about to faint.

'Bring a chair for the prince!' The queen spoke up.

A chair was brought in, as well as a fan and scented wine for Uthiyan to drink. Uthiyan waved it away, conscious of the fast that he had been keeping. 'Forgive me, Ko, it has been so long–'

'I am your brother!' The king was confused, almost angry.

Uthiyan hung his head. He was getting it all wrong. 'I did not know how you would welcome me,' he tried again.

'What do you mean?'

It all rushed out of Uthiyan then. His fears that Shenguttuvan would have been angry, that he would see him as a traitor.

The king – his brother – laughed. 'Never. No. Come, hold on to me, if you are well enough to stand, and I must show you something.'

They walked out of the tent. Outside, by the stables, lay a huge rock of granite, larger than anything Uthiyan had ever seen. 'It takes four elephants to carry that piece,' the king explained. 'I brought it back from the Himalayas.'

'What are you going to do with it?'

The king smiled. 'Build a great statue. Come, see.'

He brought Uthiyan into another enclosure, where a team of sculptors worked with clay, surrounded by rows upon rows of figurines. The sculptors leapt to their feet as they entered, and prostrated before the king.

'Here, my artisans are coming up with designs for the statue that we plan,' Shenguttuvan explained. He picked up the closest figurine, and placed it in Uthiyan's hands.

It was a tiny clay figure of a woman. Her eyes were ablaze, her hair unbound, and in one hand she clutched an anklet, and she raised the other hand to point at the sky.

This wasn't Kuttuvai, the goddess of war, for whom his forefathers had built a shrine, and whom they worshipped.

'Who is this?' Uthiyan asked.

The king smiled. 'This is Kannagi. The Kannagi of your song. We're building a statue of her, in Vanchi, one that all the people will see, to be reminded that the kings too are subject to justice.' He turned to look at Uthiyan. 'I was fascinated by this epic you have created. A story by a prince, about the trespasses of kings. By a monk, telling of a courtesan's love. By a man of the suffering faced by women.'

'You make me out to sound greater than I am.' Uthiyan shook his head. 'I am not. This is merely the tale that chose to tell itself through me.'

'Be that as it may,' the king replied, 'I have decided to celebrate your Kannaki as a goddess, to build a great statue of her in Vanchi, to remind the people and all kings after me that the first duty of a king is to justice.'

Shenguttuvan paused. 'Do you remember the prophecy? The one about you and me.'

Uthiyan smiled ruefully. 'How could I not? But the astrologer was mistaken, it did not come to pass.'

'Word came from Madurai that you were dead and a man had been executed for that crime. So we thought the prophecy wrong. But now I believe it has come true.'

'How is that possible?' Uthiyan exclaimed. 'I am monk and I have no desire to be a king ever!'

'I think we – and the astrologer – misunderstood the prophecy. I believe that the poem you have created – your song – will outlive your life and my reign. And through that poem, and not through any feat of arms or victory, your name and mine will live on.'

'Truly? You think that?' Uthiyan whispered.

'Uthiyan, I have heard your poem. And how could you think that I, your brother, would not understand? I know why you left – because you thought I would be a better king than you. How could I not know that? You are my brother, you share my blood. I have tried all these years to be the king that you would have expected of me – but Uthiyan, without you, it has been difficult. I have made mistakes, and those mistakes have haunted me, kept me awake on so many nights. If you had been there, I would have never made those, I am sure, and lives would have been saved or been better.'

Shenguttuvan moved closer to Uthiyan, and joined his hands together in a gesture of entreaty. 'So, I beg you, come back to Vanchi. Come back and be my counsel. Say to me the things that others are scared to say to a king, but that you can say to your brother. I love you, brother, and I cannot tell you how my heart is thrilled to see you after so long.'

Uthiyan shook his head. 'The life of the palace is not for me. I can not. Not the plots, the intrigues, the assassinations . . . I . . .' He felt faint again.

'Stop there, I'm not saying come to the court, or the palace. We'll build a shrine to Kannaki, where her statue will be, and you can live there. That could be your place. And I will come to you, brother, when my heart is disturbed, and when I do not know the right thing to do. That is all I ask.'

But it would not be just that. Uthiyan knew, the news would travel through Vanchi amd Musiri. People would come to gawk at him. Could he bear that again?

Something else occurred to him. He stared at the rows of figurines that surrounded him. Kannakis – so many of them. Some were curly-haired and fat, some were thin, but all fierce, all angry.

What would Kannaki the innocent village girl have told him to do?

What would Kannaki, the queen, have advised?

'They'd both tell you to go,' said a voice inside him. 'And tell you to help your brother make a better kingdom.'

And something strange happened – a hard, tight knot in his chest, a burden that he had been carrying for years, eased and unwound. Uthiyan nodded. 'There could be no greater honour or duty. I will come.'

And found himself gripped in an embrace again. 'Thank you. I thought I might never see you again,' Shenguttuvan said.

Uthiyan looked up, and saw tears glinting on the king's cheek. 'Why! You are crying!'

Mischief lit Shenguttuvan's face. He grinned. 'No brother, those are your tears.'

Uthiyan raised a hand to his face, and was surprised to find that it was true. 'I have missed you for so long,' he told his brother.

'And I you,' the king replied.

And it felt to Uthiyan that he was home.

Copyright Acknowledgements

The poems recited by Paranar in chapter 5 are Poems 144 and 145 of George L. Hart and Hank Heifetz's wonderful translation of the *Purananuru*, ascribed to Paranar (George L. Hart and Hank Heifetz, eds, *The Four Hundred Songs of War and Wisdom: An Anthology of Poems from Classical Tamil, the Purananuru*, Columbia University Press, 2002, p. 91).

The poem recited by Uthiyan in chapter 5 is taken from Alain Danielou's beautiful translation of the *Silappadikaram* (Prince Ilango Adigal, *Shilappadikaram: [The Ankle Bracelet]*, translated by Alain Danielou, New Directions, 1965, p. 38), as are the poem recited by Sattan in chapter 14 on the 'Witless Swan' (p. 39), the poem recited by Madhavi in chapter 19 (p. 45) and that recited by Kannaki in chapter 28 (p. 115).

Copyright Acknowledgements

I thank Professor Hart and Dr Heifetz for allowing me to quote from their translation. I also thank the FIND foundation for permission to use and quote from Danielou's translation.

Author's Note

A series of synchronicities led me to the *Silappadikaram*, the beloved epic of the Tamils composed by the Chera prince turned ascetic Ilango Adigal.

A chance meeting with a graphic novelist in a coffee shop got me thinking of a tale I had read as a child – the tale of Kannagi, the woman who tore off her own breast and destroyed the city of Madurai.

A month later, I found myself at a residency in Italy, in the home of the famous Indologist Alain Danielou. In his vast collection of books I searched for a copy of the *Silappadikaram* and found that Danielou himself had translated this work, as well as its sister epic, the *Manimekalai*.

I dived into the *Silappadikaram*. It began to possess me. I wanted to tell its story and began exploring possibilities of voice and plot. Initially, I had imagined a different novel. But when I reread the *Silappadikaram* a short year and a half after the Nirbhaya rape, I was struck by the relevance of this epic to our times. The core concern of the *Silappadikaram* is rage – with its potential to kill people and destroy society – and for me India in 2014 was seething with unexpressed rage. I began to fathom the depth of Kannagi's wrath – so black and intense that it caused a woman, a woman who had struggled against adversity, to wound and mutilate herself grievously, and wreak destruction on the city of Madurai – and saw its parallels in the simmering, bottomless anger of women today.

In the course of my research, I learnt that the *Silappadikaram* is merely one of many epics that focus on women, such as the Tamil stories of *Manimekalai*, *Neelakesi* and *Kundalakesi*, and *Siri* from Tulu Nadu. While they present varied points of view and espouse different concerns, all of them question our common understanding of epic literature as tales of the male heroic quest and the battle between good and evil, whether it is the Ramayana, the Mahabharata, the Iliad, the Odyssey or even the *Lord of the Rings*. But here, the epic is different, it is the quest of the heroine, often a commoner, who changes and reshapes society.

When I delved into Sangam history, I discovered many Kannagis in its literature, and this shaped my novel. For instance, the poets Paranar and Kapilar mention Kannagi in their verses, but their Kannagi is a queen.

Ilango Adigal's is not.

But it is Ilango's Kannagi who is apotheosized, transformed into a goddess – the deity Pattini – still worshipped today.

I began to fashion my own versions of Kannagi for the story I wanted to tell.

I discovered fascinating things along the way – confusions about chronology that have given rise to some exciting, imaginative theories; discrepancies in dating that have led some to believe the Cheras had a system of dual kingship.

We don't know exactly when the *Silappadikaram* was written. Some believe it was in 180 CE, based on the wonderfully named 'Gajabahu synchronism' – an instrument of chronological dating which places King Gajabahu of Lanka as a contemporary of Shenguttuvan. Other estimates date the epic back to sometime around the fifth and sixth centuries CE, perhaps even later. After the cultural and literary renaissance of the Sangam era, a veil seems to fall over history from the third to the seventh centuries CE, and this period is called the Kalabhras Interregnum. Not much survives from this period save its literature and a few historical epigraphs. During this time, it is believed that the Kalabhras defeated and ousted the Cheras, Cholas and Pandyas.

The Interregnum is seen as a dark age. Dark not in the sense of being regressive, but because we know little about it. Could it have been a time of great conflict? A time of civil war? The literature of this period reflects civil themes, a certain anti-monarchical bias, like in the *Silappadikaram* and the *Manimekalai*, indicating the growing influence of Jainism and Buddhism. Could this mean the Kalabhras were Jains or Buddhists? We do not know.

Did the Kalabhras destroy monuments? Did they destroy literature? Do the anti-monarchical aspects of the *Silappadikaram* and the *Manimekalai* – where kings and princes are unjust and societies are destroyed as a result – reflect historical realities? Is this what caused the Kalabhras to displace the Cheras, Cholas and Pandyas?

As I spent time in research, even travelling to the places featured in the *Silappadikaram*, I became obsessed with these questions arising from the gaps in our historical knowledge.

When I actually started writing, another novel emerged. It was not the tale of Kannagi or of her rage, not primarily, at least. It was about the author of the *Silappadikaram*, its creator, Ilango Adigal or 'the ascetic prince'. Legend has it that after a prophecy named him the next king, he renounced his claim to the throne in favour of his elder brother, and became a monk.

A Jain monk who wrote an erotic epic. A prince who wrote of the king-destroying rage of a common woman, and dedicated this work to his brother, a king. A man who wrote an epic poem of a woman's quest for justice.

So many paradoxes.

It was Ilango Adigal who began to fascinate me. I think I fell in love with my imagined version of him. We do not know Ilango's actual name – but I decided to call him Uthiyan, after an ancestor of his, another famous Chera king. In the process of imagining him, some part of him was embodied in me. I, a woman, a common woman, smouldering with rage, began to write about a man – a prince – and *his* rage. Across the centuries, I felt I was starting to reflect, to imitate Ilango Adigal in some sense. He wrote, perhaps, at the cusp of the glittering Sangam Age and the beginning of the Kalabhras Interregnum. Given the events of the last few years, it often feels that we are on the brink of a new dark age. According to the historian Barbara Tuchman, Ilango Adigal (or Uthiyan, as I have imagined him) was a figure whose life seemed symbolic of the complexities of his time, and so offered a 'distant mirror' to my own.

The prince ascetic and his epic offered me something else as well – a glimmer of hope. Ilango Adigal and *Silappadikaram* helped me realize that rage is necessary for justice and transformative change. Yet I do have difficulties with his text. His Kannagi is turned into a goddess, and in many ways the *Silappadikaram* affirms patriarchal notions of chastity and the duties of a wife. Kannagi does not chastize Kovalan for abandoning her for Madhavi, she merely suffers, and it is this aspect of the epic and her character that I take issue with.

But the process of working on this novel, of figuring out what a man might think and do in certain situations, taught me a great deal. It transformed my own relationships and I learnt how necessary empathy is to reconcile ruler and ruled, man and woman, spirituality and sexuality. This empathy is only possible when we step out of the roles assigned to us.

For me, this was perhaps the most valuable lesson, and the most healing one. I started writing this novel burdened by a number of wounds – the trauma of childhood sexual assault, post-traumatic stress from working in a conflict zone, warped, socially inherited ideas of masculinity and feminity, success, failure and boundless anger – that had made me cut off and deny parts of myself. These wounds are not unique; so many others carry them. Ilango served as a guide to how we must use empathy to reject binaries and accept paradoxes within ourselves. For me this is the only way we can hope, individually and as a society, to heal and become whole.

It was a difficult, challenging novel to write.

I am partly Tamil (Arni is a town in Tamil Nadu), but I don't speak Tamil. (I relied on the offices of a wonderful aunt, Uma Madan, to read me the original Tamil text of the *Silappadikaram.*) I wish I had the time and money to read more, learn the language, research more. I am not a historian, I am merely a lover of history. And I am still a novice with much to learn as a writer. I often found my skills and abilities woefully inadequate for the task I had taken up.

But if not me, who? And so, I persisted.

And here it is.

December 2018
Bangalore

Acknowledgements

If it takes a village to raise a child, it takes a couple of villages to get a writer to start on and finish a book.

This work would not have been possible without the generous aid, help and support of the India–Europe Foundation for New Dialogues (FIND). Not only did FIND invite me to a residency in Zagarolo, Italy where I came across Alain Danielou's translation of the *Silappadikaram*, but the foundation gave me a generous grant to start research. I must thank the people of FIND – Jacques Cloarec, Adrian Navigante, Petra Lanza, Sylvain Dumont, Sarah Eichner and Sofia Tarela for all their help, suggestions and support. And many thanks to my Italian publisher Roberto Calasso for recommending me for the residency. For more about FIND please do visit www.find.org.in.

This work would also not have been possible without a British Council–Charles Wallace India Trust Writing Fellowship that sent me to the University of Kent in 2015. Many thanks to Richard Alford at CWIT and Professor Alex Padamsee at the University of Kent for all the encouragement, book recommendations and conversations. Many thanks to Solomon Jayasingh for his help in getting me to the UK.

A huge mountain of gratitude to my agent, Jayapriya Vasudevan, for keeping my spirits up through this work, and seeing me through thick and thin.

I also am hugely indebted to the wonderful folks at Juggernaut: my editor R. Sivapriya, who helped this book become so much better than it was; Arushi Singh, for being so meticulous, patient and committed; and my publisher Chiki Sarkar, for believing in this book.

So many thanks to all the academics who gave me the time to talk to them and encouraged me to continue with this project – Professor Crispin Branfort at SOAS for insightful conversations and many resources, Professor Vidya Deheija for pointing me towards interesting resources and Professor Indira Peterson for advice, encouragement and friendship.

A special debt to Professor Paula Richman for her support and a friendship that has spanned decades, for a copy of her work on the *Manimekelai*, and for reading a preliminary draft of this book.

My students and colleagues at the Srishti Institute for Art, Design and Technology for letting me teach the *Silappadikaram* and Sangam poetry. Huge gratitude to Dr Geetha Narayanan for giving me a job to teach.

So many thanks to my travelling companions and friends along the way – Varun, my brother, for coming on that first trip to Madurai with me, Pavithra Srinivasan for introducing me to the history of Karur and Melmavarthur, Kuppuswamy Ganesan for bringing me back to my roots, in Arni.

Anita Ratnam for spending long hours, in different cities, discussing the *Manimekelai* and *Silappadikaram* with me.

A huge, huge thank you to many friends – Uma Madan for spending so much time reading the *Silappadikaram* in Tamil with me and for all the conversations this inspired. Arshia Sattar and Ila Chandrashekhar for putting me in touch with Uma. My neighbour Vivek Shanbhag for lending me a copy of A.K. Ramanujan's *The Inner Landscape*, which I took years to return. Harish for helping me with accommodation in Madurai. Lakshmi Chaudhry for friendship and reading a preliminary draft — helping me figure out what wasn't working. Meena Kandasamy and Krishna Udayasankar for support through the writing.

A huge thank you to my housemates – Ankita, Tanvi, Tullika and Rajeev for all the tea, coffee, food and alcohol that they provided whenever I hit a writing block (which was often).

A huge thank you to family. To Ila and Indi Chandrashekhar for conversations and support. Clare and Abhimanyu Arni for help, travel and advice. My brother Varun for coming along on a crazy trip to Madurai, Thanjavur and Poompuhar in search of Kannagi.

And to my parents, Anand and Kanchana, for much emotional support, cat-sitting and putting up with me for the last thirty-four years.

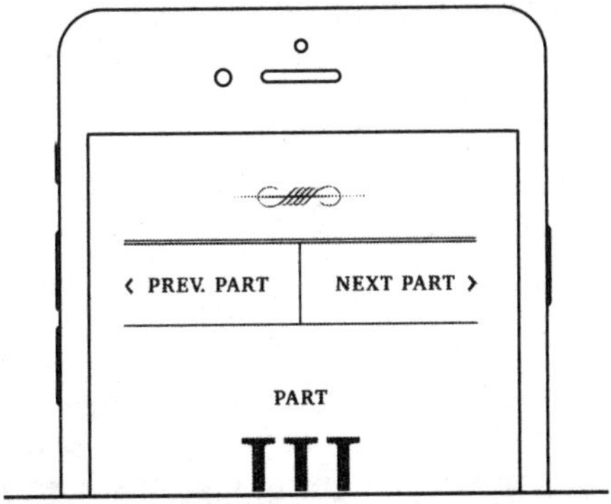

Beautiful Typography

The quality of print transferred to your mobile. Forget ugly PDFs.

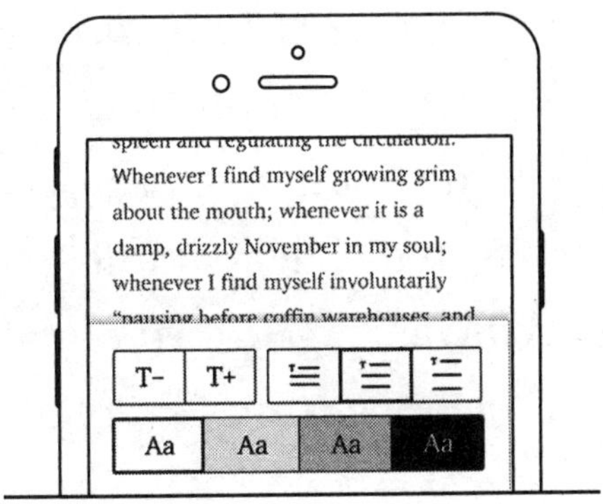

Customizable Reading

Read in the font size, spacing and background of your liking.

juggernaut.in

juggernaut.in

Ask authors questions

Get all your answers from the horse's mouth. Juggernaut authors actually reply to every question they can.

Rate and review

Let everyone know of your favourite reads or critique the finer points of a book – you will be heard in a community of like-minded readers.

Gift books to friends

For a book-lover, there's no nicer gift than a book personally picked. You can even do it anonymously if you like.

Enjoy new book formats

Discover serials released in parts over time, picture books including comics, and story-bundles at discounted rates. And coming soon, audiobooks.

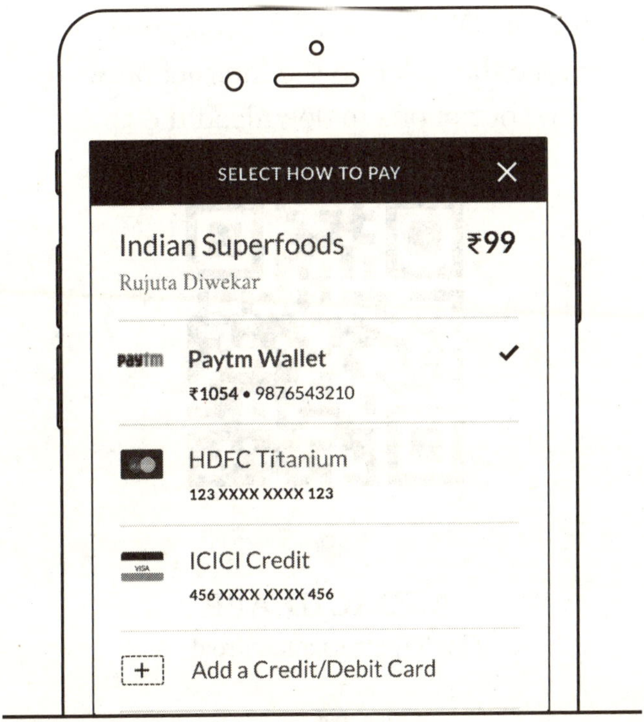

Paytm Wallet, Cards & Apple Payments

On Android, just add a Paytm Wallet once and buy any book with one tap. On iOS, pay with one tap with your iTunes-linked debit/credit card.